COWBOY CONSPIRACY
BARB HAN

TORJAKE PUBLISHING

Editing: Ali Williams

Cover Design: Jacob's Cover Designs

Proofreading: Judicious Revisions

To my family for unwavering love and support. I can't imagine doing life with anyone else. I love you guys with all my heart.

CONTENTS

1

Piper Gold lifted her right hand to shield her eyes from the blazing hot Texas sun. She had no such protection from a grandmother on a mission.

"You might be pleasantly surprised if you stick around the house for a little while," Gran said with a tone that implied she was up to no good. The wink that came next solidified Piper's reasoning for heading back to the barn to keep working. She couldn't get too mad at the sweet woman who'd been the only female figure in Piper's life.

"Is that seriously the reason you called me over here? Because you have another 'winner' to fix me up with. I thought you actually needed help with something." She made air quotes with her fingers when she said the word, winner. She also shook her head and made a show of rolling her eyes.

"I do." Gran laughed. It was good to see her smile. Piper had no idea how much longer Gran's mind would be clear or even if she would still recognize Piper's face in twelve months. Tears welled in her eyes just thinking about the medical diagnosis that caused her to upend her life and move back to Cattle Cove to face Gran's future together. Piper ducked her head and coughed, trying to hide her emotions from Gran.

"Someone will be here soon, and I thought you might want to visit with him. For old time's sake," Gran said.

"I've got work to do." Piper shot a warning look at the woman who'd practically raised her, a woman she loved dearly. "And you better not be trying to fix me up on another date with a random guy without telling me first. I've only been home four days and I'm here to spend time with you."

"No one is too busy for a gentleman caller." Gran's face broke into a wide smile as she filled the watering can, obviously pleased with herself. She shrugged, playing the innocent game.

"Gran. If I stick around here and chit-chat with a 'friend,' who will feed the horses or clean out their pens?" Right fist planted on her hip, she realized she was being a little dramatic. Piper was still reeling with how much of her life had just been flipped upside down and she hadn't had time to process all the changes. Because bad news always traveled in pairs, she'd learned that Gran's barn hand, Owen Dyer, had been called away to care for his aging mother in Fort Worth after she took a devastating fall.

Running Gran's business, COZI B&B, was supposed to be temporary until Owen could return, and then he called and quit. Hiring someone new was out of the question. Once Piper saw firsthand how bad her gran's memory was getting, she realized that she was going to be here for the long haul. Piper had volunteered to help out her gran in a heartbeat and would do it again tomorrow. She'd barely had time to unpack her suitcase and Gran was fixing her up with strangers. That part was a hard no.

Returning to the area where Piper had spent most of her childhood brought back a flood of memories. All of the good ones involved either Gran or her best friend, Declan McGannon. Gran had taken Piper in after her father was arrested and then convicted of a crime that he swore he didn't commit. She'd grown up close with Declan despite his popularity and the fact that he was part of one of the wealthiest cattle ranching families in Texas. She was quiet and kept to herself, which didn't help matters during her father's trial.

Declan was also the only one who stood by her side during her dad's arrest and trial. The two had been inseparable until her dad went to prison and Gran thought it best if Piper was homeschooled. Declan still came over as often as he was allowed between school, homework and his chores around the ranch his family owned. And then the two of them lost touch after her father was released and he moved them to Austin to get away from all the shameful stares and accusations. Being back also reminded her of all the folks who wouldn't be so happy to realize she was sticking around permanently. James Bowker would be the president of that club. She involuntarily shivered thinking about him. It was best to push those unpleasant thoughts out of her mind. Those were her father's demons.

The sun was high in the sky on a typical weekday in the fall in Texas, the temperature hovering in the low eighties…

"I'll be back as soon as the work's done," she said. Gran might be turning into a handful, but Piper loved the woman with every fiber of her being.

"Don't take too long." Gran hummed as she watered her ferns on the back porch, probably humming one of her favorite show tunes. She loved Broadway despite never leaving COZI B&B, the place she'd started with her husband thirty-five years ago.

"When you live in the best place on earth, why would you leave?" Gran's words wound through Piper's mind. Piper's grandfather had passed away before Piper could get to know him. From the stories, though, he was a great person.

In her teenage years, Piper had taken it upon herself to educate her gran on the reasons people took vacations. They were meant to recharge their batteries and try new experiences. But Gran wasn't having any of it. She'd wave her hand in the air and say that was crazy talk; everything she needed to 'experience' was right there in Cattle Cove.

It had taken years for Piper to realize Gran never left COZI because this was the place where she felt closest to the man she'd spent most of her life with—her husband.

Suddenly, the thought of losing Gran, too, struck like stray lightning on a sunny day, unexpected and dangerous. Physically, Gran was strong. Mentally, not so much. Gran chalked her issues up to becoming senile, but the doctor had confirmed there was more to it and now that Owen Dyer had to quit, it was up to Piper to help Gran live out the rest of her life in the place she loved.

Being in Cattle Cove, watching her once-fiery grandmother as she lost her mental sharpness nearly broke her heart. Since coming to COZI B&B to help Gran, Piper had been living equal parts frustration and pity. Her gran was the last living Gold after Piper's father lost his life last year.

She'd been home a few days and wasn't certain she was cut out for country life. She already missed living in Austin with its weird vibe and live music. The place was twenty-four-seven. Being back in Cattle Cove was a throwback. It was quiet unless she counted the crickets chirping—chirping that had kept her up all night the first night. Don't even get her started on how pitch black it was at COZI after dark.

The idea of Gran being forced off the property she loved if Piper didn't give up everything she knew caused a wrench to tighten in her stomach. She felt incredibly selfish feeling sorry for herself after the woman had helped Piper find her footing after her father had been arrested. Gran had also been there when Piper's father had died last year. Thinking about her gran's declining mental state added to Piper's funk. It was strange to think she would be the last Gold on her dad's side. Piper never really knew her mother. So, she had basically no relatives on that side. She'd played around with the idea of getting on one of those genealogy sites and tracing her family history. She wasn't sure she wanted to know. Piper's parents had been teenagers when she'd been born. All she knew about her mother was that the woman had handed over her newborn daughter and never looked back. Her father had offered to give over her mother's name, but Piper didn't really care. Her birth record had been sealed because she was supposed to be an adoption.

Piper's chest squeezed and her heart hurt thinking about losing the last of her family, especially Gran. Sucking in a breath, filling her lungs with much-needed oxygen, she grabbed the barn door handle and slid it open.

She loved the satisfaction of a day's work in the stables. She put her gloves back on and reclaimed the shovel she'd been using before Gran had interrupted, thinking how she needed to figure out a trip back to Austin in order to put her furniture in storage and close out her apartment. Her landlord, Briley Hope, had agreed to let Piper out of her lease after she got the call that Owen had taken off and most likely wouldn't be coming back anytime soon.

She understood the news about his own mother had come out of the blue and, of course, he should help his own family, but it didn't sit right that he'd abandoned Gran like he had. Piper was probably being overprotective but what happened to loyalty? Owen Dyer had worked for Gran the past ten years.

Piper still wasn't clear on the details of his mother's condition, only that he'd had to leave abruptly. Her heart went out to him. When she'd gotten the news about her father…

Rather than slide down that slippery slope, Piper dug the beveled end of the shovel into the pile of hay and walked it over to Rosie's stall before scattering it around. One of the best parts about being at COZI was the work. Sure, it could be backbreaking, but it was also exactly what Piper needed because work was good for grief.

After losing her father last year, she didn't want to think about Gran dying. It was impossible not to feel like everyone was leaving her.

She'd barely worked up a sweat when a loud noise startled her. She glanced around, realizing it came from somewhere behind the barn. She tried to place it but couldn't. Something faint and far off made the hairs on the back of her neck tingle. She listened for the unfamiliar sound, trying to figure it out. It wasn't a howling. It couldn't be a wolf, not this time of day. She thought about a coyote. And then she heard it again...

It made the hairs on her arms prickly. But what was it? And, more importantly, where was it coming from? Icy fingers gripped her spine at the sound. An animal? In trouble? Being attacked?

Pulse racing, she stalked over to the corner of the barn to retrieve the shotgun she'd placed there. The weapon was gone. She'd been forgetful lately with all the stress coming at her, but she was almost a hundred percent certain that she'd put her shotgun there. After being stalked by a coyote and coming close to being attacked when she lived here with Gran during middle school, she'd learned to keep a weapon handy.

This part of the country could be deadly. There were feral hogs in the area even though they didn't usually come this close to the house. She fisted her hands and planted them on her hips, staring at the wood beam where her gun should be. She issued a sharp sigh. Now she was the one losing it. Her shotgun must be in the main house. By the time she ran there and back, whatever animal was making that sound would be long gone and she'd be too late to help.

When the noise sounded this time, it was so loud and so gut wrenching that she took off toward it. She might not have a shotgun handy, but she picked up the shovel. She could use it to scare off whatever animal was attacking.

Frustration nipped as she bolted toward the sound. She supposed she had to get used to these kinds of noises.

Piper blasted out of the barn to the woods that weren't ten feet from the back door. The sounds, the wails were growing, and it was pitiful. Her heart wrenched. She heard something else too, but she was sure what it was. Something with a motor.

The animal cried out again—pain. The feral sound shot through the woods and blasted her in the chest. Whatever that animal was…

Wait, maybe there were poachers on the land. They never came this close to the B&B, but she couldn't rule them out and they were more dangerous than many wild animals.

Either way, she bolted toward the noise as she gasped for air. Running through the trees, she darted left and right, ducking branches as others slapped her in the face. The toe of her boot got caught in scrub brush and she faceplanted as the poor creature cried out in agony.

She wondered if those teenage Maddox twins had gotten loose again and thought it was a good idea to steal her boat and torture an animal. Because the other sound in the background was a boat motor.

The screams intensified. The howling intensified. The noises shot straight through her soul. She'd never heard anything that sounded so pitiful. Her only reaction was to keep running toward it.

Maybe she could scare off the attacker by yelling. She screamed, loud and wild, doing her best to be intimidating.

As she neared the lake, the sound suddenly stopped.

The trees thinned as she got closer to the water's edge. The scrub brush opened up a little more. A flock of birds flew out of the trees as she breached the line.

Her thighs burned and her lungs clawed for air as she searched for the animal, and it had to be an animal based on the sound. She white-knuckled the shovel and scanned the area for any signs of a wild hog or black bear. She'd heard they were in these parts. She saw nothing. She was one hundred percent certain this was where the noise came from, so it was confusing to get here and not be able to find it.

Was the animal dead? Had the carcass been dragged into the woods and she'd somehow missed it?

She skimmed the treetops and then dropped her gaze to the underbrush. More nothing. Her side ached from running. She bent forward and tried to catch her breath. She listened for any sounds, any whimpering, anything that could lead her to the animal. Her heart went out to it because those howls had been heartbreaking.

There was no engine-sound or boat on the lake. The water lapped up on the beach area, just like normal. There was nothing out of the ordinary. And that was just...strange.

Could she dare hope that she'd managed to scare off the attacker?

She walked around the water's edge, skimming the surface. She turned around and scanned the treetops again, searching for a predator. There was nothing. No one was around.

It was difficult to hear anything, even something subtle, as she sucked in bursts of air trying to fill her lungs with oxygen.

Piper stood there for a couple of frustrating minutes, searching everywhere and coming up empty.

She didn't want to leave any stone left unturned considering a life was a stake. She had a soft spot for animals, preferring them to humans most of the time.

After a few more frustrating moments, she concluded that whatever happened out here was gone. It was quiet now, she'd caught her breath, and she'd already been walking around for several minutes. This was a bust. She said a silent protection prayer for the animal.

Turning around, she started back toward the barn. A few steps in, a hand reached up and caught her by the ankle.

Piper gasped and tried to jerk her leg away, but the grip was too tight. All she could do was scream. And she did just that. So loudly, in fact, the sound echoed through the trees.

2

Declan McGannon stepped onto the back porch of Violet Gold's B&B. COZI was a Cattle Cove staple and Ms. Gold had been a fixture in town since before he was born. She was also one of the kindest people he knew. So, when she asked him to stop by and check a spot on her roof, he'd thrown a ladder in the back of his truck without question.

There was only one vehicle in the parking lot when he pulled in and parked. Not a good sign for how well business was going. He'd also heard about her hired hand needing to leave on short notice for a family emergency. Rumor had it Owen Dyer quit, leaving Ms. Gold in a lurch.

Declan grabbed his ladder and headed around back. The property held good memories of being here with his best friend, Piper. At thirteen, she had yet to grow into her tall frame. Her fiery hair was long and thick, but he doubted he'd ever seen it outside of a ponytail. She'd worn glasses and had braces back then. Freckles dotted the bridge of her nose and he'd thought they were the cutest things.

Considering how much he'd changed since they were kids, he wondered if he'd recognize her if she walked right past him today. Smart. Funny. She'd had a quick wit that he missed since she moved away with her father. She'd been a great buddy, and the fact they had the same sense of humor made him figure that was part of the draw of hanging out.

Piper had an amazing ability to see Declan as an individual and not just a McGannon. Carrying that last name brought expectations, considering his family was one of the wealthiest cattle ranching families in Texas. It came with a responsibility to act a certain way with folks. Declan didn't mind showing respect, especially to his elders. But his last name meant he always had to be 'on' even during his hormone-fueled teenage years that made him want to punch a hole in the wall some days as he learned to deal with pressures from outside the ranch.

With Piper, he didn't have to put on airs. He could relax and be himself. He still remembered the time he'd chased a hog away from her dog, Max, in the rain and ended up covered head-to-toe in mud as he brought her beloved pet back to the B&B. She'd met him halfway across the backyard, soaked, with rain pouring off her impossibly thick eyelashes, bringing both him and her dog into a bear hug. Missing her had caused him to push those memories down deep but it was nice remembering now.

Shame about her father, Declan thought.

"Good morning," he said to Ms. Gold as he rounded the corner and glimpsed her watering her beloved ferns.

"Morning." Her face broke into a wide smile. The twinkle in her eyes gave him pause. He'd seen that look before and it meant she was up to no good.

Being here made him wonder how long it had been since he'd seen her granddaughter. He hadn't done the math on that one recently. He'd kept a running count what seemed like forever ago. He and Piper had lost touch after her father was released from federal prison and he collected her to relocate to Austin with him.

Declan had been happy for her for the reunion. She loved her father and the town scandal had made it impossible for the man to think about settling down in Cattle Cove again. Austin was a decent drive from town, but he'd figured she would be back to visit on weekends and holidays. Much to his shock, that never happened. If it did, the visits were so low-key no one knew about them, including him. Looking back and realizing the magnitude and the mess of the situation, it made sense that her father wouldn't show his face in town again.

Piper had always been the quiet, smart one who flew under the radar, whereas him being a McGannon made him exceptionally visible. Maybe their friendship was a case of opposites attracting. All he remembered after she left for Austin was that he'd realized how much she meant to him. Considering he wasn't one to sit on a computer or be glued to a phone screen and neither was she, the two lost touch. Declan was an outdoor person, preferring a night under the impressive Texas sky to being hemmed inside a building. There was something about being in the house that made him crave his freedom. One of the benefits—and there were many—of being a McGannon was that he had access to thousands of acres of unspoiled land.

Piper's father must have been anxious to leave everyone and everything from Cattle Cove behind in order to start over. Although Declan suspected Piper and her father came to visit Ms. Gold, he'd been told to keep his nose out. A motto that was an unwritten and often spoken rule among small towns.

"Where did you say the gutter was down?" He scanned the house as he leaned his ladder against the wall, thinking he could fix the spot on the roof and then head to the hospital. His own father had had an accident in the equipment room on the ranch.

"First things first, how's your father, Declan?" she asked with a look of compassion.

"Same."

"Still in a coma?" Her brows drew together.

"Yes, ma'am." Ever since the accident, his father had been confined to a hospital bed.

"I'm truly sorry to hear that, Declan. I'll keep your father in my prayers."

"I appreciate it." He meant it, too. His father could use all the help he could get. Declan glanced up. "I'm headed that way after…"

"Oh. Well. It's over there right where you're standing," she said with a little too much innocence in her tone.

What was she up to?

He set up the ladder and climbed to the top rung. "Looks okay up here to me. Can you be more specific?"

"Well, never mind then. If it looks good to you then it was probably just my imagination." Ms. Gold returned to watering. He climbed down, confused.

"Coffee before you head to the hospital?" she asked, and that twinkle in her eyes came back.

"Sure." Was she lonely? He didn't mind sitting for a minute with her. She'd always been kind to him growing up and his turn at the hospital wasn't for another hour. He'd been going up early to get an update, but he could text in the group chat, so he did just that to let them know he might need coverage

A scream split the air. The female voice echoed, the terror reaching a deep place inside him, a protective place. A place that hadn't been stirred in a long time.

"Piper." Ms. Gold dropped the watering can in her hand.

"Where?" Why is she back? What's going on? Is she okay? His mind raced with questions as he bolted toward the trees, calling out her name. He had a general direction but didn't want to waste time after hearing the panic in her voice.

There was no response, so he called out to her one more time as he barreled past the barn and into the trees at a break-neck pace.

"Piper," he shouted.

"Over here." Her voice was barely recognizable. What did he expect? A middle school-aged kid? The still pre-teen or barely teenage buddy that he used to hang out with?

"Help," the plea came again and shot right through him.

Declan shifted his trajectory toward the sound. With a laser focus, he took off to the east. He darted deeper into the trees and zigzagged around trunks, lifting his legs high so he didn't get caught in scrub brush and lose valuable seconds—seconds that could save her life based on the urgency in her tone.

The trees started to thin, and he could see the lake fairly well in the distance.

"Where are you?" he shouted to Piper and his heart gave a little flip at the thought of seeing her again.

It took a second for her to respond, but when she did, he locked onto her location. She was closer to the lake than he originally believed, so he pushed harder. His thighs burned and his chest heaved as he cut a hard right before breaking through the tree line.

A lightning bolt struck the center of his chest when he saw her, but he didn't want to acknowledge it. Despite the expectation that time had somehow stood still and he'd find that same willowy, redheaded thirteen-year-old—unrealistic as it had been—she'd grown into a beautiful woman. Seeing her fiery red hair and impossibly soft but serious brown eyes stirred something inside his chest.

But her face was twisted with panic. She was on her knees, bent over what had to be a body, administering CPR.

"Are you hurt?" was his first question as he neared. There was so much blood—blood on her shirt, blood on her hands, blood on her jeans.

The body, the male, had a hole in the center of his chest that oozed blood. Her palms were planted just above it as she administered compressions.

"Harry Whitaker," Declan said under his breath as he dropped down beside her.

The victim's eyes were open and fixed toward the sky. His lips were blue, and his face had gone pale. It was almost like looking at a mannequin lying there. Harry was gone.

"Piper, are you hurt?" Declan scanned her body for signs of injury. Again, his heart gave a traitorous flip.

"I'm fine." The truth couldn't be further from those two words, but Declan had no plans to call her out on it. She might not be injured but she was most definitely not fine. In fact, there was so much panic in those beautiful brown eyes that he was taken back.

Declan checked Harry's wrist for signs of a pulse. There was nothing. Piper worked even harder, counting and then going back to compressions. Declan slid closer to her and took her wrists in his hands, stopping her in action.

He made eye contact and held her gaze.

"He's gone."

THERE WERE *many things to be in shock about right now. Seeing Declan McGannon again was the one that had to be shifted to the back burner.*

"No. This can't be," she said, blowing out the breath she'd been holding as she sank back onto her heels.

Time slowed and she felt trapped in an alternate reality. She looked down at all the blood. From a distance, the sound of sirens pierced the air.

"What happened, Piper?" The sound of Declan's voice washed over her, bringing her back to the present.

"I have no idea. I heard what I thought was an animal being mauled by a predator, so I ran to its defense only to find Mr. Whitaker bleeding out." She could hear the anguish in her own voice. Her heart pounded her rib cage, beating out a staccato rhythm as she tried to process the scene. She'd jumped into action trying to save him after experiencing the shock of his hand grabbing her by the ankle.

The image of him trying to speak, of him gasping for air would no doubt haunt her for years to come.

"It was so awful, Declan." Somewhere in the back of her mind, it registered that Declan McGannon was sitting next to her, all grown up and gorgeous. But she couldn't focus on it right now.

"I'm so sorry," was all he said, all he had to say to send a soothing balm straight to her heart. It was probably just their history coming into play that made her feel like the whole world might not be crumbling around her.

"You did everything you could to save him," Declan soothed.

She held onto those words as if they were the only life raft in a raging storm. Trying to stay afloat, she reminded herself to breathe. The anxiety she'd developed when her father went to prison resurfaced. She knew what to do; focus on what she could control even if that was just her breathing.

Declan stood and helped her up as he shouted directions to emergency workers. Not two minutes later, the area swarmed with EMTs and law enforcement.

Thankfully, Gran stayed back at the house and she must've been the one to call. The trek through the woods would have been too much for her and Piper couldn't even think of what her Gran's reaction would be to finding one of her neighbors on the property...a dead neighbor.

Those last words forced a slap of reality. Mr. Whitaker was dead. Granted, no one would classify the man as easy to get along with. Piper had heard her Gran talk about him when her father was alive. The man was always challenging property lines or waging a war over water rights. Piper couldn't say that she knew him personally. She had no way to judge his character. But watching him take his last breath, she couldn't help but think no one should have to die alone in the woods.

As the sheriff hurried over, Declan stepped beside Piper, effectively blocking the woman from having access.

"Declan, I need to speak to Ms. Gold to get a statement." Sheriff Laney Justice offered him a handshake. Her serious expression and calm, reverent tone caused Piper to sidestep Declan.

She offered a thank you low and under her breath, hoping only he could hear.

He gave an almost imperceptible nod and yet his defensive posture remained the same. Piper appreciated his willingness to go to bat for her. It struck a deep chord and she realized how much she missed her former best friend and having someone who had her back for a change.

Piper gave her statement to the sheriff after introductions, appreciating the fact that Laney Justice didn't treat Piper like the outcast she felt every time she returned to Cattle Cove. She couldn't blame the town. It was probably the way her father insisted on arriving and then leaving in the middle of the night when everyone was asleep that made her feel like she'd done something wrong. The two of them would sneak in for a holiday and leave almost as quickly as they arrived.

Not that she didn't understand on some level. The move to Austin with her father kicked off with a feeling of adventure but eventually caused her to feel like a criminal. Then, there was the time she'd asked to reach out to Declan. That had been a hard no from her father, along with the implication that her even asking was a betrayal, a response that she'd never fully understood. Declan had nothing to do with her father going to prison. He had to have been just as shocked as her when the former sheriff showed up in the middle of the night to arrest her father. The last thing he'd said to her was, "Keep a low profile in case someone tries to get revenge on me by hurting you."

Talk about emotional scars. They'd racked up after that statement from her father.

Gran had allowed Declan to visit, but Piper hadn't been allowed off COZI property for much. She switched to homeschooling because her father believed she'd be safer that way. Those weren't the words he'd used at the time, but she eventually put two-and-two together.

"I'll need to speak to your grandmother," the sheriff said after taking Piper's statement. It hadn't taken long to retell the events. She could only relay what she'd seen and heard.

"I need to get these clothes off," she said, thinking she wanted to burn them. There was no way she could put on this cotton shirt and jeans again without thinking about Harry Whitaker. Shock was beginning to wear off and her body started a low tremble.

"Those will have to be entered into evidence." The sheriff gave Piper the most compassionate look. Then came, "I'm sorry. It's protocol."

Piper turned to Declan, remembering her gran's suspect behavior from earlier. "Are you coming back to the house with me?"

"I'd like to," he said. Looking into those intense, dark eyes again had her heart performing a herculean summersault routine. When did Declan McGannon send her heart racing faster than a practiced thoroughbred on race day?

She tucked her chin to her chest to hide the blush crawling up her neck and started toward the house.

"Excuse me," a deputy's voice stopped the three of them in their tracks. They all turned around. "Does anyone know who this belongs to?"

With gloved hands, he held up a shotgun.
"I do," Piper announced. "It's mine."

3

Sheriff Justice turned to Piper and Declan's heart sank. The admission most likely moved Piper from witness to suspect. It seemed to dawn on her when she put her hands up, palms out, in the surrender position.

"My shotgun was stolen earlier," she said quickly. Her gaze bounced from the sheriff to the deputy and back. "I promise I had nothing to do with what happened out here."

"Where were you this morning?" the sheriff asked.

"Home. And in the barn. Gran can vouch for me," she insisted.

Declan hoped her gran's word would be enough.

"Here's what we're going to do," Sheriff Justice said. "The three of us are going to walk back to the house and I don't want either of you to say a word when we get there. I'll ask Ms. Gold if she can verify your whereabouts. In the meantime, I have to ask if you've discharged your weapon in the past twenty-four hours."

"No, ma'am," Piper's voice was strong and confident.

"Have you visited a gun range?" she continued.

"No, ma'am. I came here to help my grandmother run her business because her employee had to leave without giving notice for a family emergency," Piper continued. "He basically quit on her and I'm here to help pick up the pieces."

"I apologize in advance, but we have to test your hands." The sheriff was going to test for gunpowder residue. As long as Piper didn't discharge her weapon, she should come back clean.

Of course, being on the scene with the victim as well as being around law enforcement now could cause both of them to pick up trace amounts but law enforcement would account for that in the calculation.

"Okay. Do whatever you have to. I'm innocent and I have an alibi." There was much less confidence in Piper's tone now despite her chin jutting out. She'd done that when they were young, too. It was her tell that she was projecting confidence she didn't feel.

She had to be panicking on a fairly large scale right now.

"I'll have to bag your clothes as evidence when we get back to the house," the sheriff said.

"I'm ready to fully cooperate, but I'll tell you here and now that I'm innocent." Piper frowned. There was *a little ire backing those words, a flashback to her father's unfair verdict? Mr. Gold had sworn his innocence. As much as ranchers keep to their own and stay out of each other's business, the news about her father had been irresistible to the grapevine.*

One of Cattle Cove's residents going to federal prison for mail fraud while bankrupting four families in the process was a huge deal. Piper had denied any wrongdoing on her dad's part and Declan feared she suffered more than she let on when they were kids because of the investigation. Being pulled out of school had to have been hard. Moving away a few years later even harder.

"I've been on property for," Declan checked his watch, "twenty minutes now and I didn't hear a shot fired. I would've heard something at the house if someone had been shot out here."

"That's right," Piper agreed, adding, "I did hear something else…I heard a boat motor. At least, that's what it sounded like. I never heard a shot fired, either. But I did hear a motor."

"Okay," the sheriff said quietly. She always got quiet when she was thinking and Declan's family had had reason to notice her habits in the past few months, considering how much time they'd spent with her. There'd been more tragedy and crime surrounding the

McGannons and their land than any family should have to deal with in recent months.

Sheriff Justice turned to face her deputy. "Look for signs of a boat and let the coroner know what to look for."

"Yes, ma'am," the deputy said.

Piper followed the sheriff back to the main house. Declan flexed and released his fingers a few times to stop himself from taking her hand in his. All of his protective instincts flared at the thought Piper could be accused of murder. He may not have seen or heard from her in years, but he knew, deep down, what kind of person she was. No one could change that much without it showing in her eyes. Instead of soft brown, they'd be hardened. And hers were still that shade of honey brown he remembered.

Besides, she couldn't kill a flea if she tried. She'd refused to so much as squish a bug and she was scared to death of spiders. No matter how loudly they made her scream, she'd insisted they be caught and released outside.

The walk back was silent, and she seemed like she didn't have any idea what to do with her hands—hands that were about to be tested and were also covered in blood from performing CPR. He caught her starting to shove them in her front pockets, catching herself and then blowing out a sharp breath instead.

He hoped the sheriff had some kind of kit in her vehicle, because Piper would need her hands to change her clothes and he could only imagine how much she needed those off. How much she would want to scrub the day off. But then thinking about Piper in the shower wasn't his brightest idea. She'd filled out and had just the right amount of curves to balance out those long legs—legs he had no business noticing on his former best friend.

So much for braces and glasses. Now, she was all big beautiful eyes, creamy skin and cherry lips.

And she was in a lot of trouble if her gran couldn't corroborate her story.

Speaking of which, Ms. Gold had seen them as they emerged from the trees and was presently running toward Piper.

"Stay back, Gran," Piper warned as the two got close enough for her gran to touch her. "I'm evidence."

"What does that mean?" Ms. Gold's gaze shifted from Piper to the sheriff and back.

"I need to ask a few questions first, if that's okay with you, ma'am."

Ms. Gold nodded but her eyes told a different story. Confusion. A little fear? She'd watched her son become a suspect, and then a convict.

"Can you tell me your granddaughter's whereabouts up until twenty minutes ago?" Sheriff Justice asked.

A look passed behind Ms. Gold's eyes that Declan couldn't quite pinpoint. A mix of anger and frustration coupled with disbelief. Dread?

"Not this again, not with my granddaughter," Ms. Gold said low and under her breath, making it clear.

"I'm sorry for this line of questioning, ma'am. But can you please answer?" Justice's tone was apologetic. As sheriff, she must know the family's history.

"I know exactly where she was because she was with me," Ms. Gold stated, chin out.

Justice turned to Declan. "Was she here when you arrived?"

He took his time in answering. Staring at the grass, he said, "No."

"Because I'd gone to the barn. He must've gotten here right after I left," Piper defended.

"That's right. He came around the corner not two minutes after she disappeared in the barn," Ms. Gold said. She put her hand on her hip like she dared anyone to say anything different.

"Is that true in your opinion?" Justice asked Declan.

"It's very possible. I heard her scream not five minutes after I arrived," he said.

"See, Sheriff," Ms. Gold said. "My granddaughter was with me most of the morning."

"Gran, you don't have to cover for me. I didn't do anything wrong and we both know it. I was in the barn earlier in the morning and Gran called me over. Said she had a surprise." Piper's cheeks flushed as she looked at Declan and his heart gave another one of those traitorous flips. "So, technically, I wasn't in the house or with Gran all morning. But I was working in the barn and had my shotgun with me. When I went to get it because of…what I thought was a predator preying on a small animal…I went to grab it before investigating and it was gone."

"Do you always carry a shotgun around with you?" Sheriff Justice asked.

"Ever since I was almost attacked by a coyote. When I go out on the land, I go prepared," she said. "And that includes the barn."

"Was anyone in the barn with you this morning?" the sheriff asked.

"Not that I know of," Piper admitted.

"THE GUN WAS NOT in her possession the entire morning, Sheriff. We both know any lawyer could tear a case like this to shreds," Declan warned. Best case scenario, he could stop the sheriff from arresting Piper and then call his family's attorney for a referral to a criminal lawyer.

"Right now, Miss Gold is a witness. As such, I need to get as much information from her as I can while the incident is still fresh in her mind. But I also have a murder weapon that belongs to her and a victim on her family's property." Sheriff Justice didn't have to explain her actions to Declan, but he appreciated her for making where she stood clear. "Follow me to my vehicle. I have a GRS kit there."

Declan started to follow but was stopped by the sheriff, who put a hand up.

"Just Miss Gold," she said.

Nothing inside him wanted to listen to Sheriff Justice. But Piper would be better off if he did. So, he tamped down the urge to be by Piper's side. Instead, he moved beside Ms. Gold where the two of them could keep watch over Piper and the sheriff.

The sheriff pulled a kit from her vehicle and had Piper hold out her hands. Justice collected samples from the back of her right hand, focusing on the thumb and forefinger, and the webbing in between. Next, she took samples from Piper's clothing.

"There's so much blood. Is she hurt anywhere?" Ms. Gold asked in a frail voice.

"Not her. By the time I got to her, she was performing CPR on the victim," he said.

Before Ms. Gold could formulate another question, the sheriff placed the evidence inside the vehicle. The pair walked back over.

"I'll go inside and bag these clothes for you, Sheriff," Piper said.

"It's best if I go with you." Justice's voice was calm and steady. Not a hint of apology but no judgment, either.

"Oh. Okay." Piper seemed to catch onto the reason, and it had nothing to do with making sure she didn't try to escape.

Letting evidence out of her sight would be a mistake that a seasoned sheriff wouldn't make. She might not have decades under her belt, but she was proving, time and time again, to be good at her job. He was learning to trust her.

"Declan said there was a victim," Ms. Gold said. Her voice rising in agitation. "Who?"

"Harry Whitaker," Piper spoke up, taking a step toward her gran before catching herself. Close contact was a bad idea and especially while she was wearing evidence that could keep her on the witness list.

Her gran gasped before bringing her hand up to cover her mouth.

"What is it?" Piper's forehead creased with concern and her brows drew together. She still had a dotting of freckles on the bridge of her nose that had somehow morphed from adorable to sexy on her.

Gran held a finger up as she mouthed, oh-no, a few times. She put her hands up to her mouth and dropped them a couple of times as she turned and headed toward the back porch while mumbling something unintelligible. Her distress was easy to see as she dropped her hands to her side and then brought them up to her face a couple more times before reaching the porch.

Before she'd walked away, her eyes took on a vacant look. Piper clearly had noticed. She shot Declan a look of despair.

"Gran, what is it?" Piper's question fell on deaf ears.

"Ms. Gold," Sheriff Justice said. Again, the elderly woman didn't listen. Either that or just didn't respond. Had she slipped into an emotional place so deep that no one could reach her? The thought brought a frown to Declan's face. This wasn't characteristic for her and he became concerned something was wrong.

"I forgot to mention this…" Her voice trailed off as she moved to one of the rocking chairs and retrieved something…a phone.

She hurried over to the sheriff. "I meant to tell Piper about this and forgot."

Declan had heard rumors that Ms. Gold's memory was slipping. Gossip being what it was, he didn't take it too seriously. He was starting to believe there was something to the talk as he looked at her distraught expression.

"I'm such a ninny. I don't know how it could've slipped my mind. It's been going on for weeks now." She held out her phone toward the three of them and made eyes at the sheriff.

The screen was black.

"Gran?" Piper's concern was evident in her tone.

Declan had to force himself not to put an arm around her like he'd done so innocently in their youth or take her hand in his for comfort.

"What?" Gran looked genuinely confused before checking for herself. "Oh. Well. How'd that happen? It was just on."

She pressed her thumb against a button and the phone came to life.

Declan studied the text messages from Harry Whitaker as a sinking feeling formed like a heavy fog, weighing down on him.

I'm coming for you. I'm taking what's mine. You'll get what's coming to you.

The messages went on and on as Ms. Gold scrolled through them.

"How many of these are there?" Sheriff Justice asked.

"I'm not exactly sure. Too many to count." She shrugged. "I ignored them when they first came in, figuring he would go away."

"You didn't think to call my office?" Justice asked.

"I didn't think they were a big deal. You know cranky old Harry Whitaker. I figured he was all bark and no bite, blowing off steam," she admitted. "But then the threats followed and that's when I asked him to stop."

"You should have told me, Gran. I could have made them stop. I could have reported him and blocked his number," Piper said. "You don't deserve to be treated like this, especially not by a jerk like…"

She seemed to think better of finishing her sentence under the circumstances. Declan couldn't agree more. He'd been the one to come up on her while she was trying to save Harry Whitaker's life. She'd been trying desperately to save him. Declan had witnessed her efforts firsthand. In fact, he'd been the one to take her wrists in his hands…

That made him think of something. "Sheriff. I grabbed Piper's wrists to stop her from performing CPR on someone who was already gone. If she fired that shotgun, I should have residue on my hands, as well."

The sheriff nodded, but she didn't tear her gaze away from the screen. Her concern was written on the creases in her forehead.

A picture was emerging. Harry Whitaker had threatened Piper's grandmother, and then he was murdered by Piper's shotgun. Her grandmother was her alibi and her doctor would have to testify to her faulty memory if called to the stand.

This didn't look good.

4

"**I**s there any chance I can get out of these clothes?" Piper asked the sheriff. She was feeling sick to her stomach and figured the shock was starting to wear off. Her body started that slow tremble again and she needed to wash the blood off her before she threw up. Bile burned the back of her throat and an overwhelming need to scrub every inch of her body overcame her.

"Of course," Sheriff Justice said. "I'll follow you."

Piper took the lead with the sheriff right behind her. Declan and Gran followed them inside but stopped in the kitchen as she heard Gran asking him if he wanted a cup of coffee.

The sheriff followed Piper upstairs and to her suite on the second floor. Justice asked a few more routine-sounding questions as Piper undressed and dropped her outer clothing into the paper bag the sheriff had opened. She wrapped a towel around herself before washing her face and hands in the sink.

Looking in the mirror, she realized she had blood in her hair.

"I need a shower," she could hardly contain the emotion building inside her, threatening to bubble over and spill out in the form of hot tears.

"I'll be downstairs, speaking to your grandmother." Sheriff Justice spoke quietly and the respect in her voice struck a chord with Piper.

"Thank you. I'll be quick."

True to her word, she showered, dressed and was back downstairs in less than ten minutes. The temptation to stand under the water and scrub her skin until she felt clean again and like she'd washed off the horror of what she'd experienced had been its own force—a force that she'd had to fight against for fear the sheriff would come back to check on her. Piper needed this ordeal over with and she also wanted to know what other questions the sheriff was asking. And then there was Declan. Being with him again was balm to her soul. He'd jumped to her defense with the kind of dedication missing in her life for years.

In the kitchen, the sheriff was seated at the bar height table with seating for four that was at the opposite end of the room. The spot had the best views of the barn and used to be one of her dad's favorites. She couldn't count the number of times she'd walked into this room early in the morning to find him there, cup of coffee in hand, staring out the backyard.

Chin to chest, she ducked her head to hide the emotion welling in her eyes at the memory. She missed her dad like crazy.

Declan immediately stood up and walked over to her. He clasped their fingers and she ignored the electric impulses vibrating through her hand and up her arm from contact. He'd grown into a beautiful man with his dimpled chin, day old scruff and incredible and intense blue eyes.

He would laugh if he heard himself described as beautiful, but he was. Beautiful. He'd filled out that tall, skinny frame. He had to be six-feet-five-inches.

Being with him again tipped her world on its axis and caused her pulse to race. She only hoped he couldn't feel her reaction to seeing him again through his fingertips.

"Do you want coffee?" he asked.

She shook her head. "Thank you, but my hand is already shaking."

He nodded, confirming that he could feel it, too. At least this way she could blame the day's horrific events.

And then there was a spark in his eye. "Didn't you used to drink some kind of tea when you needed to calm down after a big test?"

She smiled even though she was pretty sure it didn't reach her eyes. It was sweet that he remembered a small detail like that.

"Chamomile. And technically, it's an herbal infusion," she said, and she could feel her smile expand despite her somber mood. Being with Declan brought a peek of sunlight into what had been one of the worst days of her life, and she'd had more than her fair share of those.

He smiled in a show of perfectly straight, white teeth. "You used to tell me that, too."

Warmth spread through her.

"I was a brat," she said, remembering how she used to go around correcting his English. "Sorry about all that."

"It was cute."

So, why did she wish he'd described her as something else?

Piper chalked her weird mood up to the stress of the day. Declan had been her best friend for a time and, clearly, still wanted to be there for her in a time of need. The only other person who'd had her back in life was Gran. Her father had been too broken after serving time in prison to be there for Piper, even though he'd tried.

"I can heat water in the microwave if you point me to a cupboard." Declan made a move to where the measuring cups were stored, and her hand felt cold the minute he let go. He grabbed a measuring cup and filled it with water before heating it in the microwave.

She retrieved a teabag. Tea was a lot easier to say than herbal infusion. After she tossed the bag into the cup, Declan poured hot water over it.

"Teamwork," he said with more of that warmth in his voice. Warmth that traveled all over her, awakening a part of her that she'd tucked away a long time ago. Trauma in a young person's life, like the kind she'd experienced when she was barely a teenager, had a way of leaving a permanent mark. One that was burned into her heart, etched into her soul.

Maybe it was being at a tender and impressionable age, but her father's arrest, followed by her being pulled out of school, had shaken her to the core. Declan was the only person who still came around after her father's conviction. Her gran's business had suffered as bookings became few and far between. Although, Gran would never tell it that way.

"It's nice to see you again, Declan." She said the words quietly, so only he would hear even though she meant them as if she stood on top of a building and shouted them from the rooftop.

"I think your gran set me up," he confided with a twinkle in his eyes. "Called me to see if I could come over and fix a spot on the roof. Speaking of which, remind me to put my ladder away."

"There's nothing wrong with the roof," she said quickly. Gran really thought she was being sneaky;

Piper had known her grandmother was up to something. Couldn't say that she was disappointed. Seeing Declan was the sun on a day that had been nothing but rain.

"When did you get back to town?" he asked.

"A couple days ago," she said.

"What about your father? Is he coming?"

She shook her head and steeped the tea, studying it like it was a cheat sheet before final exams. He seemed to catch on.

"I'm so sorry, Piper. When?"

"He passed away last year." She shrugged like it was nothing, but it was purely a defensive move. "After he got out, things were never the same. He was...broken by the experience. He threw his back out while serving time. Said it happened at the gym when he was trying to work off all the stress. Said he went too far and permanently damaged his nerves. After that, he was on prescription medication. He must've taken more than he realized one night and mixed it with a couple of drinks. I tried to take his car keys away. He was too strong."

She lifted her gaze, expecting to see judgment in Declan's eyes. Instead, she found compassion.

"He was dealt more than his fair share," he said quietly, reverently. Those few words coming from *someone who had been so important to her at one time held a strange healing power.*

She didn't question it, didn't want to question it. All she wanted to do was let that power settle over her. Free her?

Declan brought his hand up to her face and lifted her chin until she brought her gaze up to meet his. Critical mistake but she was going all-in at this point.

"You have, too. And you didn't deserve it."

Piper took in a sharp breath and ushered in the woodsy, campfires and outdoors scent that was uniquely Declan.

Suddenly, it was like she was looking at him for the first time and her chest could scarcely contain her thundering heart.

DECLAN TOOK A STEP BACK, unsure of what was happening between him and his former best friend. Strange, new territory that neither seemed ready for. He'd already lost her once and, now that she was back in his life, he didn't want to lose her a second time over an attraction that couldn't go anywhere.

Relationships came and went, and he'd had his fair share, as he was certain Piper had. Although, nothing in him wanted to think about her with another man in that moment.

He'd get there. He had to. This time, he wasn't letting her get away so easily. He'd missed their friendship, their compatibility and the easy way they had with each other. He missed his best friend.

So, no, he had no plans to mess it up with a physical attraction. Although, he couldn't deny she'd grown into a beautiful woman. And there was a freckle just above her lip that he wanted to capture with his lips more than he wanted air a few seconds ago.

Declan smiled to himself, and then gave a mental head slap. Piper coming home was the best thing that had happened to him in years. He needed to leave it at that.

"Tea's probably ready." He recovered his normal even-keel temperament.

This close, he noticed how crazy thick her lashes were and how they hooded a pair of the softest honey brown eyes. His heart took a hit when she blinked up at him.

So much for even keel.

Clasping their fingers together after she picked up her mug, he asked, "Are you ready to finish talking to the sheriff?"

"As ready as I'll ever be," she said.

They walked over to the table and he could feel her hand tremble in his. He started to let go but she tightened her grip.

"I'd better head back to the office so I can arrange for the lab to pick up the evidence." Sheriff Justice stood, acknowledging them both with a nod. "If you think of anything else, call my number."

Piper's gran promised she would. "I'll walk you out."

"Actually, I don't mind doing it. I have a few questions for the sheriff," Declan said.

"Oh, okay," Ms. Gold seemed surprised. She might not realize the legal drama going on with his family.

He followed Sheriff Justice outside to her vehicle before saying, "I heard you brought my Uncle Donny in for questioning again."

"That's right," she confirmed. She opened her SUV door and secured the bag of clothes in the seat before turning around and leaning an arm against the opened door.

"And?"

"You know I can't discuss the details of an ongoing investigation with you, Declan," she warned. "I would if I could. I have nothing to gain by shutting you or your brothers out."

"Seems like you've been asking him a lot of questions. That's all." Since his uncle had been with Declan's father when the accident occurred and it was widely known that Uncle Donny wanted a bigger piece of the pie after blowing his inheritance, the whole situation was suspect considering Donny had been in the same room when his brother ended up taking a fall that led to a coma.

"I can confirm that is true." Her lips formed a thin line. "Is there anything else you'd like to ask me, knowing that I can't comment on an ongoing investigation?"

"I guess not."

"How about this. I promise to keep you and your brothers informed if there's anything I can say."

"Deal." What else could he say?

She climbed into the driver's seat and he watched as she pulled away.

Declan hurried back into the kitchen.

Piper blew out a slow breath as she claimed a seat. "My father used to love this spot. Said that if there was heaven, it was right out that backyard."

Declan didn't remember much about her father. He basically only knew what townsfolk had said. What he did know was that Piper thought the world of the man. There seemed to be a special bond between daughters and fathers. Although, he didn't know from personal experience. Declan wasn't a father and had no plans to be despite the fact his own family was a close bunch. He, his brothers and his cousins had all grown up on the McGannon family ranch together. The bonds were tight.

"I miss him," she admitted before turning the tables like she was trying to shake off a heavy coat that came with dwelling on her loss. "What about your family?"

"It's been crazy lately. A few of my brothers are married. A couple of them are waiting for Dad to wake up to make things official," he said.

"What do you mean by wake up?" She set down the mug and ran her finger along the rim.

"You haven't heard?" he asked, surprised her gran hadn't mentioned it. But then, Piper did say she'd only been there a few days.

She shook her head.

"Dad had an accident in the equipment room. He lost his balance and ended up with a head injury." He studied her for a long moment, wanting to tell her the rest. Everyone danced around the topic at home. It was probably the close bond the two of them had shared as kids that had him wanting to tell her more.

"What else?" She always had an uncanny ability to tell when he was holding back. The fact she still could sent a wave of comfort and familiarity running through him—a dangerous combination for someone sticking to the 'just friends' route. "You're not telling me everything."

"Uncle Donny was with him," he said.

"Since when is he back in town?" Shock widened her eyes and played out on her features. "Never mind that question. I'm sure a lot has changed since I left."

"Your grandmother didn't keep you posted?" His curiosity got the best of him and he went ahead and asked.

"No." She shook her head. "Once my dad was released, he wanted to get away from Cattle Cove, from the rumors and gossip. If the two of them talked about people from here, I never overheard it. Even at a young age, I figured out that my dad wanted a fresh start. Bringing up this place seemed to make him hurt that much more."

"I never believed he defrauded those people out of their life savings," he said.

"You're probably the only one," she admitted. "And I'm grateful that you didn't turn your back on me while I waited for his release. You probably just came here out of charity but you—"

"I came out of friendship," he quickly corrected not bothering to mask the hurt in his voice. "And when did I ever treat you like a charity case?"

She clamped her mouth closed like there was something else she wanted to say but stopped herself. After a thoughtful pause, she said, "I was about to say that you never once made me feel like charity."

"Because we were friends." He stopped short of saying best friends, but it was true for him. He couldn't speak for her, but he still felt that same connection even now, like the years between them had dissipated and they could pick up exactly where they left off.

He took a sip of his coffee, thinking how her family's circumstances must have made for a lonely life for her. On the occasions he'd been allowed to visit her at COZI, they'd been too busy goofing around outside to talk much and he figured she'd speak up when she was ready. Then, she moved away before she ever got the chance.

Looking back, he couldn't help but think he'd made the wrong call in staying silent on the subject. Leaving her to believe he thought of her in the same manner others had.

Then again, after the black eye he'd given Jordan Palmetto for talking trash about her after she was pulled out of school, it was possible people only spoke about her behind his back. Declan had been a lot more hotheaded back then.

Maturity helped him realize using his fists wasn't the best way to settle an argument. That and the fact he'd always lived in the spotlight. Everything he did was gossip. Having the last name McGannon was reason to be proud. His father had built a legacy of honesty and hard work, of being fair. Declan had felt like a real jerk for tarnishing his family name, even briefly and in light of the fact Jordan had it coming to him. No one put down Declan's best friend while he was in earshot.

"I'm really sorry to hear about your dad, Declan. He's a great person and he doesn't deserve what happened to him," she said.

Her heartfelt words touched him in a place he'd tucked away a long time ago. "Thank you, Piper."

"I don't think I ever thanked you for sticking by me," she said before leaning over and giving him a kiss on the cheek. She hesitated and it took everything inside him not to act on that instinct from earlier to claim that freckle above her lip.

5

N*ot one person in more years than she wanted*

to count had caused electricity to ping through Piper's body the way physical contact with Declan just did. She chalked it up to nervous energy from being in Cattle Cove again. Between Gran's medical condition and the horrific events of the morning, she was off balance. Her emotions were on the edge and it didn't take much to stimulate them. Whatever just happened between them wasn't as special as it felt right now. It was most likely seeing his friendly face that stirred her heart in ways she'd never experienced than a real attraction.

"Tell me more about your uncle." She desperately needed to redirect the conversation.

Declan shrugged, leaned back in his chair and picked up his coffee mug. After taking a drink, he said, "You know Uncle Donny. He's around and has his hand in things but it's always been my dad who kept his brother in check, so my uncle has been off the rails."

"That must be hard for your cousins," she said.

"Yes." Declan laughed. "Well, I guess you really haven't heard any of my family's recent news. I have a brother I never knew about."

"You're joking." There was no way. "Did your dad remarry?"

"Nope."

"Out of wedlock? I have no judgment there but he's from a different generation and that seems out of character for your dad," she surmised.

"The guy is six months older than Levi." Declan's lips compressed.

"Your dad had an affair?" She couldn't contain the gasp that came out of her mouth. "What did he have to say about the situation? I'm sure there's a logical explanation. I mean, your father loved your mother and he didn't exactly have a reputation for being unfaithful."

"That's true. As soon as the DNA test came back as a match, we accepted Kurt into the fold. Dad still doesn't know what's going on and can't exactly explain in his current condition."

She put two-and-two together. "Why do I think your uncle has something to do with this?"

"Bingo." He issued a sharp breath. "A few of us believe he brought in the mystery brother to pull the attention away from himself and that has all of us on edge. Kurt seems like a decent guy. He had no idea who his father was and by all accounts didn't care. Uncle Donny called him to the hospital one day. Kurt showed for his little girl, but he didn't make the best first impression. Now, that we've had a chance to get to know him, though, he's a good person. Levi and A.J. were first to welcome him into the family."

"But not you," she said. Declan had always been the wait-and-see type.

"He's growing on me. The kid is cute. She's all curls and chubby cheeks." His response caused her heart to give a traitorous little flip. It was a dangerous reaction to someone she cared about and didn't want to lose.

"I bet you're a good uncle," she said.

"I'm a great uncle. Fatherhood…that one is not for me. But being around the little carpet crawlers can be fun."

Well, now her heart really clenched. The image of Declan married with kids wasn't something she really wanted to think about.

"What about you? There has to be someone special in your life." Suddenly, the rim of her coffee cup became real interesting.

"Not really." He shrugged broad shoulders and the cotton material of his shirt pulled against a chiseled chest. "I've been around…dated quite a bit. Haven't found anyone special enough to lock down with, if you know what I mean."

His admission caused a wave of relief to wash over her. She said it was because she wanted to think that she still knew him as a person and not that she was personally invested in his relationship status.

And then he turned the tables. "How about you? Anyone light those little fires inside you?"

If only he knew. The one person she'd felt that instant zing of attraction strong enough to light anything inside her had been him.

"No one special at the moment." She wasn't sure why she felt the need to add those last three words, but that's what she did. Maybe to deflect the way heat crawled up her neck and caused her cheeks to flush when she talked to him about dating.

Now that they'd gotten that out of the way, more of that heat filled the space between them. But she had other, more immediate things on her mind than her heightened feelings for her best friend. And she needed to redirect the attention away from the goose bumps on her arms at being in the same vicinity as Declan.

He was beautiful, she thought for the third time today.

It was Piper's turn to lean back in her chair if only to put a little more space between them. She took a sip of her chamomile as she looked out onto the expansive lawn that her father had referred to as heaven on earth. He was right. The place was perfection, and, despite Gran's financial troubles, Piper was determined to roll up her sleeves and figure out a way to ensure Gran got to live out the rest of her life on the land she loved.

"What brought you back to town?" Declan asked.

"Did you hear about Owen Dyer?"

He nodded.

"His leaving put Gran in a lurch." She glanced around to make sure Gran wasn't within earshot. "That, and the fact Gran's mind has been slipping lately. The doctors are saying it's more than forgetting little things here and there, like she'd have me believe. Like I did believe until I came to see for myself."

"She seemed agitated earlier when she forgot to tell you about the text messages she'd been receiving from Harry Whitaker," he pointed out. "Have you seen her like that since you've been home?"

"A couple of times, especially in the kitchen. She'll be in the middle of cooking and forget where a certain pan is or where she keeps her spices. I've seen her become very flustered and she's hard on herself when she has a slip. And that's just what I've seen since coming home a few days ago." She'd first noticed the memory blips on the phone less than a year ago. Gran had laughed them off in the early days, but she was *becoming more and more frustrated as her memory slips worsened.*

"How long do you plan to stay?" he asked. The look behind his serious blue eyes intensified and her heart clenched.

"As long as I need to." She turned her face toward the window. "She deserves to live out her life here, Declan. She loves this place. I'll do whatever it takes to make that happen for her."

"What can I do to help?" His question was so immediate, so honest.

"You're already doing it," she said, risking a glance at him.

His eyebrows were knitted together. Confusion stamped his features.

"You're listening to me. You're being my friend." She reached out and touched his hand despite knowing it would be a big mistake. And it was. Her skin sizzled where it touched his.

"I'm here. And I'm not going anywhere," he said.

Those words felt a little too much like a promise. She knew better than to read too much into his offer.

And yet, there she was. Her stomach freefell like she'd just gone base jumping.

DECLAN STARED *at his hand where it connected to Piper's for a long moment. And then he shook it off. She needed a friend and he needed to stay focused. If, for some unknown reason, her hands came back with powder on them—not that he thought she'd shot Harry Whitaker because he didn't—she'd be in serious legal trouble. He needed a clear mind if he was going to be a help to her.*

"I didn't do it, by the way," she said, as though she could read his thoughts. She couldn't. They used to do this all the time. Get lost in their own thoughts while in the same room with each other and end up thinking the same thing.

"I know."

"I can't prove it yet," she stated, and he could hear the low-lying panic in her voice.

"I know that, too. That doesn't mean we won't be able to prove it and besides, the evidence will show that you're innocent."

She shot him a look and he understood exactly why without her needing to explain.

"The timeline doesn't work with you as the shooter," he said.

"True," she conceded but she wasn't convinced.

"Plus, you won't come back with enough residue on your hand," he said.

"Which doesn't mean they won't try to pin the crime on me."

"I personally didn't hear a shotgun and I would've from here. I heard you scream, and your grandmother can testify that she didn't hear a shot," he said.

"The crazy thing is that I didn't hear one. Wouldn't I have heard it?"

"Did you hear anything?" he asked.

"Yes. Like I told the sheriff. I could've sworn that I heard a motor. Sounded like a boat," she said.

"Well, the deputy is probably still on the scene and he'll most likely find something. A trail. The victim's body had to have been dragged or carried. They'll find footprints along the shoreline. There would have to be mud since the crime occurred near water. If two people carried a body there'd be deeper impressions from their shoes. As long as they follow the evidence, they'll be able to prove your innocence."

"Gran's doctor will have to be honest about her memory issues if he's called to the stand, and I'm

certain he would be if this investigation goes south for me," she admitted.

"The timing of me showing up should help with the timeline," he said.

Despite the fact that everything he said was the most logical thing, she stared out the window, eyes huge, filled with disbelief. And when he really thought about it, of course she did. Her father hadn't exactly gotten a fair shake in this town. She'd sworn her father was innocent and Declan had no reason to doubt her.

Sometimes, evidence was wrong, or a jury made a mistake. A prosecutor took a shortcut. So, he wasn't too surprised when he really thought about it and she didn't get overly excited that the evidence would clear her name.

"Some people will say the apple didn't fall far from the tree." She shook her head.

"Let them."

She shot him a look that stopped him right there.

He put his hands in the air in the surrender position. "Okay. I see your point. Your family doesn't exactly have a history of getting a fair trial in Cattle Cove. But I can contact our family's attorney, and get a recommendation from her for an attorney to represent you. The truth will come out."

"I don't exactly make the kind of money I would need to hire a top caliber defense attorney. Gran is *practically out of money and the small nest egg I have saved will only get us by for a little while until I can straighten out the books here. I'm just starting to dig in the financials and see all the mistakes she's made. I don't know how I would be able to afford an expensive lawyer." The words came out in a rush and she barely caught her breath in between.*

So, he slowed down and took a minute before continuing.

"I have more money in my bank account than I could ever spend." He blew out a breath and held up a hand to stop her from interrupting him. "All my expenses are paid, and I literally have nothing to spend it on. It's collecting dust in my bank account."

"I couldn't do that. I couldn't let you do that. It's too much, Declan. And that's your future you're talking about."

"Why not? You'd be doing me a favor. It would help me feel better about inheriting all this money that I didn't earn. What good would it be if it didn't help the people I care most about?"

She compressed her lips and brought her hand up to cup her forehead. That was her tell that she was at least listening to him. It wouldn't be fair for her to be convicted of a crime that she didn't commit because she didn't have enough money to mount a decent defense.

"I still can't."

"Give me one good reason," he said.

"Because I would never be able to repay it. And how would that be for our friendship?"

Declan heard what she was really saying loud and clear. He respected her for it. Piper was used to earning her own way. She wasn't the type to take a handout. "How good would it be for our friendship if you were wrongly convicted of murder?"

Yes, he was being harsh putting it out there like that. He could only hope the shock of hearing those words could penetrate her pride and help her see reason.

"How awful would I feel if I could've helped you and didn't?" He kept going when she didn't immediately argue. "I can't lose you again, Piper. Not if I have the means to help."

"I'll think about it, Declan." There was no conviction in those words.

"Promise me," he urged.

"Okay." She leaned forward and put her head in her hands. "You're right. I can't afford pride right now. I'll consider letting you help me but only if there's a way to figure out how I can pay you back."

"Definitely." Good that she was beginning to see reason. Her life might be hanging in the balance and he'd meant what he said. Money was just numbers in a bank account if it wasn't used to help others. Declan *didn't take his upbringing for granted and he didn't throw money around lightly. He'd been taught to respect what had been given to him even if he never had developed a comfort level with that amount of wealth.*

In his job, he'd never had to. His horse didn't care if he was rich or broke. His dog, Red, never showed a preference. All she cared about was getting her kibble on time. The simple fact of the matter was that he loved being out on the land, being in nature and around his animals. Mother Nature sure as heck didn't care how many zeroes he had in his bank account.

One of the many qualities that had drawn him to Piper all those years ago was that she didn't, either.

It didn't seem like much had changed and that made him a lot happier than it probably should, especially with the way his chest squeezed every time he looked at her.

6

The tea in Piper's mug had gone cold. It was long past lunchtime. She doubted she could eat a bite of food. Her stomach lurched thinking about trying to force it. But Declan might be hungry.

Before she could ask, he stood up.

"More tea?" he asked, motioning toward her cup.

A question loomed between them. Would Piper need to tap into the McGannon family fortune to keep herself out of jail?

Talk about a daunting thought. Defense. Lawyer. Murder charges. Not exactly words that came to mind when she'd made the decision to move in with Gran last week.

At some point, shock would wear off and she might begin to process what happened. There was no way it could've already considering the fact her mind could scarcely wrap around the fact Harry Whitaker was dead. He'd been a jerk to her gran, but no one deserved to be killed. Did he send anger-fueled texts to others or just Gran? If he was the type to lash out to anyone he didn't like, there could be a long list of people who wouldn't mind seeing him go away permanently.

"What do you know about him? About Mr. Whitaker?" she asked Declan.

"Not a whole lot. You know me. I tend to keep my head down and my nose in McGannon ranch affairs. I don't go nosing around where I don't belong. I didn't even know you were here or coming back into town." He shrugged a shoulder like it wasn't a big deal but there was something in his tone of voice that made her believe otherwise.

There was enough there she felt the need to address it before it became the elephant in the room.

"Honestly, the decision to pick up my life and move here happened so fast. Gran came to Austin for a doctor's appointment a couple of weeks ago, and I got the news about her memory. Not that I hadn't already noticed her mind slipping but when I was back in Austin and doing my own thing, I'm embarrassed to say it was pretty easy not to notice. Or, you kind of notice but it doesn't quite register if that makes any sense." She felt the need to explain and realized she was probably going overboard to ease some of her own guilt about not figuring it out sooner. Then, there was the fact she hadn't reached out to him.

It just became really hard after what happened and seeing the way everyone judged her family. Moving to

71

Austin, she felt like she was putting a painful past behind her in a lot of ways and making a fresh start. Everything here reminded her of having her dad taken away.

She remembered mentioning wanting to see Declan to her dad and the hurt in his eyes when he'd given a hard no for a response. The past was off-limits as a topic. Her dad had been through so much and she didn't want to see him hurting anymore. She especially didn't want to be the cause of his pain. It took years to realize that she was causing her own self pain in trying to make someone else happy. The crazy part was that if her dad realized, he would've told her not to. That understanding came with age and more experience.

"Maybe we can go out once the deputy is gone and investigate the area. I seriously doubt Sheriff Justice is going to give us a whole lot of information about an ongoing murder investigation, so we might have to do a little digging ourselves," Declan said, and she noticed his change of topic.

Gran walked into the kitchen, looking like she was flustered.

"Have you seen my keys?" she asked Piper.

"Which set?"

"My car keys, of course."

"What do you need them for?" Piper needed to have the conversation with Gran that she'd had with her doctor, which was that they needed to very seriously think about retiring her driver's license.

"I've got to pick up bread. I was going to make sandwiches for lunch, and I can't make sandwiches without bread." She searched her pockets and came up empty.

Piper glanced over at the kitchen counter where Gran always kept the bread and saw the fresh loaf that she'd run out to the store to pick up last night by Gran's request.

"You know what? I saw that we needed bread last night and decided to run out to the store to pick some up." She motioned toward the loaf, deciding not to mention the fact that Gran had specifically asked Piper to go to the store last night to pick up a few items, including the bread.

Every time she brought up a memory slip to Gran, she got more and more agitated with herself. Piper realized how tricky these waters were going to be to navigate over the next…however long it was going to play out. She would take all the years she could get with her beloved grandmother.

Her heart fisted in her chest at the thought of life without the vibrant woman and role-model. To this day, Piper associated being in the kitchen, baking, with unconditional love. Every holiday, every birthday, Gran could be found in the kitchen making pies or baking cookies, making something from scratch. It was such a throwback compared to Piper's adult life in Austin where her kitchen wasn't much bigger than a postage stamp. She couldn't remember the last time she boiled water on the stove let alone brought out a pie pan or cookie sheet.

Did she even own a muffin pan?

Her life in Austin was take-out meals and grocery store baked items. She waited in line for the best food, which didn't necessarily mean the most expensive. She ate on more park benches than at her dining room table because she would grab fifteen minutes for dinner when she could get time.

Piper never felt more loved and accepted than when she was with Gran in her kitchen. The thought that her beloved grandmother could get to a point where she didn't even recognize Piper anymore was too much to process.

She took in a deep breath, trying to stave off the anxious feeling closing her chest and making it feel like her rib cage was shrinking.

Her father loved her dearly and she realized that without question. It was different growing up with a single dad. Gran was a grandmother and had to step into the mother figure role. She was also Piper's best friend when she was little and now that she was older, as well.

As Piper sat there and looked at her gran, smiling at the person she adored most in this life, a deep sadness came over her at the realization she had no idea how much longer Gran would remember who she was.

"I'll just make those sandwiches then." She thrust her fists in the air like in triumph. "I made some of the best chicken salad on this side of the Alamo." She directed her gaze at Declan with that undeniable twinkle in her eye. "Are you in?"

"I think we ate the last of it yesterday." Piper popped to her feet and moved to the fridge. She opened the door and showed Gran the empty shelf where the homemade chicken salad had once been.

"Well, will you look at that." Gran smacked her hands together.

"We can have this ham and cheese…throw some lettuce on it. Do you want mayo or mustard?" Piper asked, hoping to redirect the conversation before Gran got flustered again.

"A little bit of mayo sounds good to me. I could cut up a tomato," Gran said.

"Or I could do it," Piper offered.

"Same here. I love mayo on a sandwich with tomatoes." Declan was suddenly by Piper's side, helping pull out ingredients.

"Looks like we're having cold cuts today," Gran declared, and Piper was relieved the change of plans didn't seem to upset Gran or knock her off balance. Two mornings ago, Gran had been thrown into a tailspin over misplacing her watering can.

Piper shot a side look at Declan, who gave a slight nod of acknowledgment. Not only was she losing the woman she loved and admired, but there was no way a court would accept Gran's testimony.

DECLAN HELPED MAKE sandwiches in assembly-line mode. He saw Piper's point about her grandmother's memory issues. There was no jury in the world who would believe she could recall time and facts clearly.

Time of death and his time of arrival were Piper's best possible defense along with the gunpowder residue test results. His was the only trustworthy alibi. He also caught the look of desperation on Piper's face when her gran was with her at the fridge.

The trio made plates and then brought them over to the four-top table. Ms. Gold poured sweet teas, and they chatted easily about the weather and how much Austin had changed over the past thirty years, becoming less weird and more mainstream with chain restaurants dotting the landscape.

After they finished eating, Ms. Gold clapped her hands together and said, "It's been quite a morning so far. I believe I'll lie down for a few minutes so I can get my afternoon bookkeeping done with fresh eyes."

"Have a good nap, Gran."

Ms. Gold wagged her finger and winked, the spark back in the woman's eyes. "You two enjoy whatever it is you're going to do." She practically pranced out of the room, much to what appeared to be Piper's mortification.

"I'm so sorry," Piper said the minute her grandmother was out of earshot.

"You don't have to be. It's kind of adorable." He chuckled.

"Until she's trying to set you up with every single person in the county." Piper picked up dishes as the green-eyed monster took a jab at Declan. He tried to convince himself that he had no right to feel that way and yet the feeling packed a little bit more punch than he was ready for.

"Who has she tried to set you up with so far?" He could hear the twinge of jealousy in his tone and had to chuckle at himself. "I can tell you who might be worth pursuing."

Declan almost couldn't believe he just said that, but he had. It was out there. He couldn't take it back despite wishing he could reel that comment back in.

Piper issued a sharp sigh. "Apparently, there's a new guy in town by the name of Brody Axel. I thought he was the one Gran was trying to set me up with today. Do you know who he is?"

That red blush from earlier crawled up her neck, flaming her cheeks and giving that creamy skin of hers a rosy hue.

"No one knows about him. He doesn't come to town much. Maybe every other week to pick up his mail and never during the day. I don't think he's your type. In fact, I think you should stay really far away from him." He didn't even like her considering talking to or meeting up with a guy who moved into a new town and made a point of staying under everyone's radar.

Brody Axel was the kind of person who went out of his way to avoid people. He had a post office box in town for his mail and Declan had heard someone ran into the newcomer at one o'clock in the morning.

"I didn't know much about him but apparently Gran said he asked Owen if I was single." She shrugged.

"Haven't you only been home for like four days?" All Declan's warning systems flared.

"Yeah. This time. I've been back a couple of times before to check on Gran after my dad passed away last year." Her voice held the sadness of losing someone she loved. He could only imagine what it must feel like watching the only other family she had start down a road of dementia.

"You've been back to town?" Before he could let himself get too riled up over that, the fact that she'd come back to town without once letting him know she'd be back, he reined himself in. "Or more importantly, how did he know you were here?"

"Gran said he knew Owen and the two talked a lot. She said he stopped by to see Owen in the barn sometimes. She said she mentioned me a couple of times. I personally have never met the guy. Gran said he's good looking and that he works out." She shrugged casually, unaware of the daggers piercing his chest.

But about Brody. Declan figured the guy was tall enough to be a McGannon, and broad. It was clear he worked out and probably played high school ball. Declan couldn't verify whether the guy was attractive. He looked a little rough around the edges and not at all someone Declan could see Piper going on a date with.

"I imagine to some people he might look okay. I don't see you with...that...with someone like that. He's always rubbed me the wrong way and I couldn't tell you why. Just a feeling, and all that secrecy." Declan was busy enough on the ranch and, like he'd mentioned before, he didn't really stick his nose in other people's lives. And yet someone who lived on the

79

fringe of society, who'd moved to a new town without really getting to know anyone, seemed at least a little bit suspect.

Most people moved to rural areas for the relative safety and the community feeling that could still be found in small towns. Others moved to escape a past or start over. Or, because they were doing things that they didn't want neighbors around to see.

Brody Axel struck Declan as the shifty type.

"Promise me that you won't go around him without me or someone else around. Someone stronger than your grandmother. I don't like the thought of you going anywhere near that guy, especially because no one seems to know anything about his background. Unless your grandmother figured it out or he told her," he said.

"Nope. Not a word. She said he moved here based on Owen's recommendation. The two of them weren't best friends but they did know each other. She thinks that maybe they worked together in the past. Brody traveled a lot for his work in construction and Owen said this was a reasonable place to buy land and have a house." Her eyebrow shot up and he figured it was because he'd maybe laid it on a little thick.

That had been intentional on his part because he could not stress enough that he didn't want her anywhere near or alone with Brody Axel. At least until they knew more about his background and they figured out why he'd really settled in Cattle Cove.

Declan made a mental note to ask Miss Penny, Aunt Penny to a few of his brothers. She answered to both after stepping in to raise Declan and his brothers along with his cousins after their mother passed away. She was the closest thing they had to a mother.

Despite them being grown men now, she had become family and still ran the house. Of anyone, Miss Penny would have information on Brody Axel if there was any knowledge to be had.

Declan had every intention of figuring out what Brody's move to town really meant and the motivation behind it. What was the real reason he'd shown up a few months ago and bought property? That brought up other questions and his mind bounced back to the case at hand.

Another question weighed on Declan's mind when it came to Harry Whitaker's death. Motive. Was there anyone else who had something to gain by his death?

"I'm sorry about not reaching out to you," Piper said, and her voice was so low that he almost didn't hear her.

"No explanation needed." He tried to shrug off the insult and make it seem like it didn't bother him. And it shouldn't. She didn't owe him a reason for her actions. They'd been best friends when they were kids, not even old enough to drive a car let alone strike a lasting bond. Relationships like those rarely ever stayed intact through adulthood. Right?

So, why did his heart want to argue that what they'd shared had been special? It clearly couldn't have been all that 'special' to her if it was so easy to leave behind without a backward glance.

The fact she'd drifted in and out of town recently shouldn't cause a knot to form in his chest, either. Declan needed that slap of reality to put their friendship in perspective. They could keep it casual. He was offering her the same help he would offer anyone else who needed a hand up. Piper was a decent person and didn't deserve what had happened to her family, what was still happening to her family…

Hold on a minute. There was at least one person in town that he could think of who might want to exact revenge against her father. Setting up Christopher Gold's daughter as a murderer would be one way. Since her father died, was she the next best thing?

7

"What do you remember about your father's case?" Declan asked Piper.

"I've blocked out as much of that as I can, to be honest. I'd have to go back and look at files to get specific information. That timeframe is pretty much all a blur. I was pretty young and I'm not sure I remember all the details correctly from back then. You know?"

"Do you have the files here?" Declan asked.

"Yes. Somewhere. I think, maybe in Gran's office. Mine and Gran's office now." She crossed her arms over her chest and studied him. "Why?"

"At first, I thought maybe someone grabbed your shotgun and found Harry Whitaker, shot him and then dragged him onto your property so that they could get away. What I'm thinking now is…what if that wasn't the case? What if the person handled it that way on purpose? What if they knew your habits and knew you'd take your shotgun to the barn with you? What if they used that knowledge to set you up for murder?" His question seemed to strike a chord.

Her hand came up to cover her gasp.

"I guess I hadn't really thought of that as a possibility. It could be. All that happened a long time ago. I don't even know what happened to the families who got involved with my dad. I know he was the only one who served time for it." She issued a sharp sigh. "I mean, it is possible they are seeking revenge. My dad's dead. He died last year. Didn't they get the ultimate revenge?"

There was a lot of fire and ire in her voice. He couldn't say that he wouldn't have the same reaction if his family was in that situation.

"Besides, I always thought my dad was set up to take the fall. In private, he always insisted he was innocent. Maybe he had evidence that could have proven his innocence but didn't use it."

"Here's the thing. From everything I've ever learned, heard or saw about a murder, it always comes back to motive. There's motive, means, and opportunity. Someone has to have the motivation to want to kill somebody and gain something by that death. Then, there's the means. You had to have been available at that time and you had to have physically been able to pull it off. You also would have had to have a weapon. And then there's opportunity. This crime, if it is a conspiracy to exact revenge on your family or send you to prison, then we have to consider opportunity. The window wasn't bad. Somebody came

84

and got your shotgun this morning from the barn. You were doing work and then you went, by your own account, to talk to your gran. Who, by the way, was apparently trying to set you up with me. There's no arguing her good taste," he teased, trying to bring a little levity to a heavy situation.

There was a tickle in his chest about the thought that maybe Gran didn't want her with Brody after all. He continued, "So, this person had the opportunity to take your shotgun and kill Harry on your property. You heard the boat engine and maybe they had to bring him. They had to be far enough away for no one to hear the shotgun. Harry's property on the backside does butt up to COZI B&B land."

She was nodding her head as she listened. "Let me get a notebook. We can maybe write some of this down." Piper went to a drawer and located a notebook and pencil. She came back over to the table and stood as she put the tablet down. She wrote the word, Revenge. In the center of the page, she wrote, Harry Whitaker. Below his name she wrote, threats to Gran. She drew a circle around Harry's name. Across the top of the page, she wrote, motive, means, and opportunity.

"You know, I bet I don't even have to go back to the files. I'm pretty certain we can make a phone call or two and figure out who else was involved with my father," she said.

"I know exactly who to call." Declan fished his cell phone out of his pocket and pulled up Miss Penny's contact information. He tapped on her name and held the phone to his ear.

She answered on the second ring.

"Everything okay?" she asked. He heard a hum in the background. Car engine?

Okay was a relative question but he understood what she meant. "I'm all right. I have a question for you, though."

He could hear the sound of the road in the background.

"Are you driving? Is this a bad time?" The last thing he wanted to do was cause her to get into trouble behind the wheel.

"No. Not at all. I'm on my way to the hospital." There was an emotion present in her voice that he couldn't quite pinpoint, but it seemed familiar with her lately.

"I don't want to distract you while driving," he said.

"You're fine. Hawk is driving."

Declan noticed that the ranch foreman and Miss Penny had been a little bit more joined at the hip over the past couple of months. At first, he thought it was solidarity's sake after his dad's accident, but they seemed awfully close now. They had worked at the ranch in different capacities for more years than he could count. It wasn't his business, so he let that fastball slide right past him without taking a swing.

"Do you remember the Golds?" he asked.

"I sure do. Such a shame. You and Piper were so close." She made a tsk noise. "That takes me back to when you were in middle school. You were so young."

"We sure were. Practically babies," he agreed. "I'm here with her right now and we have a question…"

"Oh."

Declan just let that surprised reaction slide right on past. It was the second one.

"Would you mind if I put you on speaker?" he continued, trying not to skip a beat.

"Sure. That's fine with me."

Declan put the call on speaker and set the phone on top of the four-top table.

"Hi, Miss Penny," Piper said.

"Piper Gold. It is still Gold, isn't it?" Miss Penny's voice suddenly became awkward.

"Yes, ma'am. It's still Gold."

Declan ignored the burst of hope in his chest that came with the admission. He'd already knew she was single and yet there was something very right about hearing the words again. And that was ridiculous because he was being oddly possessive over a friend.

"You said you had a question for me?" Miss Penny asked.

"That's right," Declan confirmed. "You remember what happened with Piper's father."

"I sure do. I am so sorry any of that happened to your family, Piper." The compassion in her voice seemed to resonate with Piper. More words that seemed to allow her to exhale a little bit more.

"Thank you, Miss Penny. It means more than you know, hearing that from you." It was almost as though Piper started breathing a little easier, like some invisible vise had been locked around her chest and she finally found the release valve.

It was probably selfish of him, but he hoped he'd had a similar effect on her.

"Do you remember if there was another family involved in that?" Declan asked.

"Yes, I remember very distinctly one of the families who was very outspoken about what happened and that was James Bowker."

THE NAME JAMES BOWKER sent ripples of frustration through Piper. It also kind of shocked her into reality a little bit more. "I heard my father talking to Gran about Mr. Bowker after my dad was released. Dad spoke about him in hushed tones and seemed to make sure I didn't hear anything."

Declan nodded to her and then turned his attention to the screen. "Thank you, Miss Penny. You're an angel. Hawk..."

"Yes, sir."

"Take good care of her."

"Roger that, sir."

Declan ended the call after Piper said her goodbyes but not before Miss Penny made Piper promise to stop by the ranch. She hadn't been out there in ages and it had always felt like a second home. She had a lot of happy memories flooding her in thinking about times on the ranch with Declan and his brothers, all of whom were honest and kind. She'd add badass to the list if someone tried to pick on someone they cared about.

Thinking about the ranch was a blast from the past to happier times when she lived in Cattle Cove with her father. Gran lived right up the road at COZI and they pretty much knew everyone in town. Piper wasn't one hundred percent certain if that town had made her feel completely unwelcome, except for Mr. Bowker and his family, or if she'd felt guilty on behalf of her dad. All she'd known was that her world had been turned upside down. She was no longer allowed to go outside *unattended. That made her suspicious and caused her to look over her shoulder. It had made her feel like everyone was against her and her father.*

Clearly, there were people who were on her side and, looking back, she wished that her family had leaned into that support a little bit more rather than isolate themselves.

She and her dad had taken up residence on the third floor of the B&B and Gran had limited guests to the second floor. She'd taken a financial hit that she'd eventually recovered from. But now, her finances were a little bit of a mess based on the peek she'd taken at them. It was something Piper needed to straighten out.

"Do the Bowkers still live here?" she asked Declan.

"Not to my knowledge. Again, I'm not an expert on all things Cattle Cove. I want to say they've been gone for a few years. I think after Morgan, the youngest, graduated high school and went off to college they moved with family outside of San Antonio. We probably shouldn't trust my memory on it, though," he admitted.

She wrote the name James Bowker under the word, Revenge. She added, Did Dad hide something or know something?

"We have a name. If the motive is revenge, which seems like a reasonable motive, all we need is means

and opportunity. But, in setting me up, what exactly would they have to gain?"

"It could be their way of metering out their own justice. We can notify the sheriff. Although, I'm certain she knows what happened with your father and hopefully she's already looking into that possibility. If we came up with it in the space of an afternoon, her list is probably twice as long already." Declan covered her hand with his and that's when she realized hers was trembling. "Would you want to go back out to the site by the lake? I think I heard a vehicle pull away while we were on the call with Miss Penny and I'm guessing it belonged to the deputy."

"I don't think I'll ever be ready to go back to that place again," she started. "But if it will help us figure out who did this faster, I'm willing to do almost anything at this point."

Declan nodded and she appreciated that he was willing to be close to her and stay, especially with his workload.

"It didn't even occur to me that you probably have a million things to do at the ranch. Are you sure you don't mind being here?" she asked.

"I'm here for as long as you need me to be. With the caveat that I will have to take off if Dad wakes up." He glanced at the clock on the wall. "I will have to run home here in a little while to feed Red and I need to let my family know I'll be out of pocket for a while."

"Red who?"

"My dog."

She blinked at him, unable to hide her shock at the fact he'd given his dog the nickname he'd had for her in middle school.

"The two of you haven't met, but she's been with me since some jerk dumped her on a country road while still tied to her cage. She was a baby, around five months old according to the vet."

Anger ripped through Piper. "Poor baby."

"I know. Sometimes, I don't understand people. I'm not going to lie about that one."

She couldn't agree more with that statement. People had always confused the heck out of her. That wasn't entirely true. She'd loved her childhood in Cattle Cove up until her father's arrest. She realized ever since then she was always waiting for the other shoe to drop. Had she been going through life not willing to risk anything? Including her heart? Because of that shoe?

There was something about a life-changing event or being around death that made a person introspective. She was really inside her head and needed to get out of it for her own sanity's sake before she got caught up in the same old spin cycle again. The one that left her tired and frustrated when she focused on the wrong that had happened to her family. Reliving it never changed the outcome and wouldn't bring her father back. And yet, it was hard to let go.

"Yeah, if I could come face-to-face with the jerk-off who thought it was okay to drop off a puppy on the side of the road still tied to her crate that was left open…the guy didn't even seem like he stopped, he probably just slowed down. But, yeah, if I could get five minutes alone in a room with him, I'd show him exactly what I thought of his negligent and criminal behavior…his choices." There was so much fire in Declan's eyes when he spoke. It was easy to see how much he loved Red. No surprise there. He'd always viewed himself as a protector of animals. Now that she really thought about it, so did his brothers and cousins. She figured it was part of a rancher's blood to love the land and want to take care of creatures that were smaller than them.

"Ready?" Declan stood and tucked his phone inside his front pocket. He caught her gaze and studied her like he needed to see that she was going to be okay.

"As much as I'll ever be. And I'm ready to get answers." She couldn't imagine facing a trial like her father had. She couldn't imagine being convicted despite knowing full well that she was innocent. And she couldn't fathom spending time behind bars for a crime she didn't commit. Her father had gone to jail for two years before he'd been released on good behavior.

Murder?

Somehow, she didn't think the jail timeline would be the same. The very real thought that she could go to jail for a crime she didn't commit rocked her to the core.

"What is it?" Declan asked. He reached for her hand and clasped their fingers. Again, she was caught off guard at just how much her hand trembled.

"What if what happened to my father happens to me?" Just saying those words out loud sucked all the air out of the room.

Declan tightened his fingers around hers. Warmth spiraled through her and yet she knew better than to let it comfort her under the circumstances.

"I'm here to tell you that I'm not going to let that happen to you. I promise." There was so much fire and determination in his eyes she almost believed him. She wanted to believe him.

But even a friend with a powerful last name couldn't guarantee that she wouldn't end up behind bars.

8

"**M**ind if we make a pit stop before heading out there? I just realized that if Miss Penny is on her way to the hospital, I need to swing by the house to take care of my dog." Declan asked Piper as he led her to his truck. He needed to pick up Red and besides, he wanted her to meet his furry best bud. Working with Red by his side made the long days and hard work more pleasurable. And Piper's stress levels were through the roof. A quick diversion might give her a chance to settle before facing the scene of the crime again.

"Sure. Anything to avoid going back to that place a little longer sounds good to me," she admitted.

"Hey, if you don't want to go back that's certainly understandable. I can grab Red and the two of us can check out the area. I give you my word that you'll be the first to know our findings." He didn't want her to feel compelled to go if it wasn't something she could stomach. And he sure didn't want to be the one to cause her more distress. Given their history and close relationship in the past, he wanted to be the one to render aid, to give her a sense of security she'd clearly lost after her father's trial and later conviction. And to give Cattle Cove back to her as a home—a place that she'd once loved.

He couldn't imagine having everything familiar taken away from him, especially not at a young, impressionable age. And maybe he wanted to make up for lost time or the fact that he'd been too immature to realize how much pain she must've been in. Heck, she might not have realized it herself. Kids were so in the moment. He was guilty. And maybe it was the fact that he was losing his own father, bit by bit, that had him wanting to restore someone's sense of family.

"I know you wouldn't hold anything back from me, but I need to go back for myself. It's hard, don't get me wrong, but I'm trying not to overthink it. We both know I'm capable of grinding it out mentally. But I need to clear my name. Does that make sense?" she asked.

"Does to me." There was a lot of honor in what she'd said. In not shying away from something because it was going to be hard. She was the type to look trouble square in the eyes and dare it to come at her again. He respected the trait in her even though he could acknowledge that it sometimes led to more trouble.

"I'd like to meet Red."

Declan smiled as he opened the passenger door for her. He opened the door, not because she couldn't do it for herself but those were the manners he'd been brought up with. Considering himself a person of tradition and nostalgia, he hoped the chivalrous acts would always be welcomed. If not, there was no way he would force them on someone. But, plenty of people like Piper still seemed to appreciate the gesture.

"Thank you," she said, before climbing into the passenger seat.

"You're welcome." He moved around to the driver's side and reclaimed his spot. The B&B was half an hour's drive from the ranch. He figured this would be a good time to catch up on what had been going on in Piper's life and maybe offer a little distraction for her.

"So, what is it that you do aside from dropping your life at a moment's notice to help out your gran?" he asked as he navigated onto the gravel road.

"I used to work for Billie Joe's."

"The Billie Joe's?"

She laughed and it was musical.

"The one. I book musical talent for them."

"Sounds like an interesting line of work," he said.

"It is if you like catering to musicians." She laughed again and the sound traveled over him.

"I also set up their backstage quarters and made sure whatever requests they had were fulfilled. Sometimes the bigger the name, the crazier the requests. Like, some have to have a specific brand of water or type of blueberry. I had a lot of interesting requests for boxed cereal." She shifted in her seat and pinched the bridge of her nose like she was trying to stem a headache even though there was a lighter quality to her tone.

He should've offered ibuprofen before they left the B&B. Clearly, the shock of the day was wearing off and the toll it was taking on her was starting to show.

"Sounds like an exciting job where you'd meet a lot of new people." The jealousy ripping through him was another thing that caught him off guard, thinking of her surrounded by famous men.

"You'd think. Most of my job was done over the phone and the internet, making sure everything was perfect before a band came was pretty high on the list. Funnily enough, it was then my job to disappear just as quickly. Or, at the very least, not be seen. That was a big part of the deal."

"I thought you'd have more contact," he said.

"It was nice. You know me. I'm not exactly one who wants to parade out into the spotlight, even before all of that happened."

Declan was beginning to realize just how much what had happened to her family, to her father had colored her life.

"You never were one who wanted to be the center of attention or have all eyes on you," he agreed. "Remember that time our English teacher was going around the room, picking on people to read out loud?"

"To this day," she said.

"You probably had the highest grade in English and were one of the best readers, but you literally shrank behind Thomas Decker trying not to be seen." He remembered like it was yesterday.

She made a show of shivering. "That is so true."

"I guess some things never change."

"People rarely change." There was a hint of melancholy in her voice.

"What happened to your father afterward? If you don't mind my asking."

"Are you kidding? You of all people knew him."

"He was a good person," he said.

"And a good father," she agreed. "Or, at least, he was. He did his best. After he served time and came out of prison, everything was different. He was different. Broken."

"Your father was a good person. He didn't deserve what happened to him and I couldn't be sorrier."

"That means a lot, Declan. Thank you. And what Miss Penny said a little while ago touched my heart."

"Miss Penny is about as good as they come."

"That's the truth. She was like a mom to me, too, in many ways. I did spend a lot of middle school on your ranch."

"Or here at your gran's B&B. I have a lot of good memories from this place."

"Yeah? Name one," she challenged.

"Let's see. How about that time you were sick, and I wasn't allowed to come see you, but I wanted to make sure you were okay and bring you history notes? Your gran thought that was fine, but she didn't think it was a good idea for me to see you. What did I do? I climbed up three stories and knocked on your window."

She laughed and it sounded like the real deal, which made him happier than he could remember being in a long time. It quickly died and she got so quiet all he could hear was tires on the road.

"Declan, I can't go down for murder. Not just because I didn't do it. But, because, I saw how broken my dad came back. He'd given up and I can't blame him. I think he only hung around for as long as he did after his release so that we could have a little more time together."

"I said it before, and I'll say it again. I couldn't be sorrier, Piper. He didn't deserve the fate that was handed to him."

"I can't help but think about your father, too. Another good man who should be out on the land he loves and not in some hospital bed in a coma. I'd like to see him at some point if he's allowed to have visitors." Those words filled Declan's chest, causing his heart to squeeze.

"He would like that," Declan said. "I think my dad always cared about what happened to you."

"What about you?" She turned the tables on him. "I see that you became what you wanted."

"Yes. Working the family business was always what I wanted." Coming from such a large family, Declan couldn't imagine not having endless family around. It occurred to him that Piper had her father and her gran. A little voice in the back of his mind reminded him that she'd had him, too. But he'd been so innocent or naïve that he hadn't realized how small her circle was in the past. It had never dawned on him just how much she needed a friend. Part of him wanted her to know that now. "I missed you when you left."

He white knuckled the steering wheel as he navigated onto the road that led to the ranch.

"You did?" The surprise in her voice caught him off guard. He thought she understood his feelings for her better than that.

"Crazy thing is, I've thought about you more times than I care to count over the past few years and I have no idea why it never occurred to me to reach out. I guess I figured that maybe you'd moved on and found happiness." That sounded pretty lame coming out of his mouth now even though it was one hundred percent true. "Any chance you can forgive me?"

"NOT A CHANCE." Piper laughed. She reeled it in the second she realized Declan hadn't gone along on that journey. "I'm just kidding. It's just been such a heavy day and I'm pretty sure I lost my mind hours ago. I'm sorry." She blew out a breath. "I don't think I can go there about us not staying in touch. It was hard enough at the time and just as much my fault. Not that you're on any sort of social media because I did check a couple of years ago."

Her attempts at humor had fallen pretty flat. It was a bad joke anyway. The day was definitely wearing thin on her. The thought of what they'd be facing next after picking up Red weighed heavily on her despite getting a break every once in a while.

Declan nodded as he pulled into the long drive at the ranch. He got through security and drove them on the long road toward the main house.

The ranch was incredible and impressive. Massive probably wasn't a big enough word for it. To the left of the main house was a parking lot and behind that an impressive barn. There was a decent sized yard behind the house and a full-sized baseball diamond. Mr. McGannon had it built after Ryan showed a propensity for the sport. Back behind the yard was a cattle pen.

Being here, back on the property brought back a flood of memories of her and Declan on the ranch. There was such an innocence about that time period before her childhood ended and she'd had to learn about court trials and defendants.

Declan parked and hopped out of the driver's seat. She appreciated the chivalry of having doors opened for her. Yes, it was a bit of a throwback, but she loved that about Declan. So, she waited for him to come around and open the door. He did and held out an arm for her to climb out of the cab.

She glanced around the place that felt so much like home. The fact the house, barns and property hadn't changed comforted her. It gave her a sense of consistency. It was the same majestic and beautiful landscape.

"Wow, Declan. Not much has changed."

He shrugged his shoulders. "Not a whole lot of changes around here. Although, I say that, and we've added quite a few family members into the fold in recent months."

"I can't even imagine that," she admitted. "I mean, I have a little bit of that with Gran and COZI. It must've been really great to grow up here, surrounded by so much family. I can barely imagine. It was just the three of us for so long and now it's down to two. Although, you saw Gran's mental state. It's not good." She ducked her head, chin to chest, to hide the emotion welling in her eyes. She didn't do that whole 'tears' thing. Not that she looked down on anyone who did. She couldn't count the number of times she wished she could have a good cry and let her emotions out; she'd become too much of an expert at holding them in, so that even when she wanted that sweet release it never came.

"I don't know if it makes you feel any better, but I can say that growing up in a house with my five brothers and five cousins, all boys, meant there were a lot of sweaty, smelly socks around. I can tell you that much."

Well, now she really laughed and some of the stress of the day rolled off her. There was just something about Declan that made her feel like everything was going to be okay despite evidence to the contrary. She knew better than to get too comfortable in the feeling because her last name was Gold, not McGannon. Golds didn't have the same kind of magic around their name that the McGannons did. But then the

McGannons had money and position in the community. Those were things that came with more privilege and were far more valuable than she'd realized growing up.

Don't get her wrong, there'd been food on the table, and she'd had decent clothes on her back. She couldn't have asked for much more than that.

Declan linked their fingers once again and she almost pulled her hand back from the heat that pulsed through her from the point of contact. She let him lead her to the barn where they stopped in front of an impressive set of doors.

He flung the door open and a gorgeous dog came bolting toward them, tail working double time. Piper definitely got the appeal of dogs. They were bright and always happy to see people. She worked long hours at the club and told herself that was the reason she hadn't gotten a dog. She'd said that it wouldn't be fair to an animal to leave it alone all day and most nights. Watching as Declan dropped her hand and then took a knee to greet his dog, seeing the joy in both of them when they met, she wondered why she'd let herself work so much that she hadn't been able to get one of her own.

"She's beautiful," she said.

"Yeah?" He scratched her behind the ears. "Red, this is Piper. Piper, this is pretty much the best dog in the whole world in my one hundred percent biased opinion."

Piper squatted down beside him and Red's overenthusiastic leap, along with a very wet tongue, knocked Piper off balance. She put a hand down, but it wasn't enough to stop herself from falling over and the red dog licking Piper's face.

She'd only known Red for all of a minute and she already loved this dog.

"Here, let me help you up." Being this close to Declan, it was impossible not to take in his features. His face was hard. Hard eyes. Hard lines. Hard jaw. Everything was hard except for his lips and those were almost impossibly full.

It would be so easy to close the distance between them and lean in for a kiss.

9

"She's beautiful."

Declan couldn't agree more with those words and his heart swelled in his chest at hearing them from Piper. He reasoned she had always been important in his life and her opinion mattered more than most.

"She's a good girl, aren't you?" he said to Red, refocusing his attention so he could get a handle on his attraction to Piper. This close, it would be so easy to close the distance between them. It wasn't far. It wouldn't exactly require building a bridge.

Declan issued a sharp breath. It was really good to see Piper again. Better than he wanted to admit, even to himself. His gaze traveled over her face, memorizing all the little details like she might disappear tomorrow.

At almost exactly the same moment, the two of them leaned into each other. They met halfway and stopped within an inch of each other's lips. With a sharp sigh, he closed that last little bit of distance between them and captured her lips.

She shifted her position to face him and brought her hands up to loop around his neck. Their eyes met for a split second and absolute thunder fired off in the back of Declan's brain. The kiss was a rain shower in a drought. Except the heat. There was so much electricity firing between them, causing his pulse to skyrocket.

A gesture that was intended to offer comfort to a friend sure had heated up, lighting up his senses and waking his heart in the process. He cupped her face with his hands to position her mouth for better access.

Suddenly, the earth tilted on its axis and the ground moved. Declan stood, bringing Piper to standing with him. She encircled her arms around his neck, her body flush with his. Her full breasts pressing against his chest.

There was an urgency to both of their actions now as her fingers tunneled into his hair. She tugged and pulled, creating a battleground of sensations inside him. A sexy groan released from her mouth, that he captured.

His thoughts spun to the point of out of control. This was Piper. His one-time best friend. She needed him and was most likely reaching out to remind herself that life could be normal again. He didn't want her to regret kissing him later, so he drew on all his strength and pulled back.

His chest heaved and he noticed that hers did, too. And in perfect rhythm with his to boot. So, how was that for maintaining a sense of calm and control?

His body wanted to act on its own accord and reach out to her. Plant his lips against hers again and see where it took them.

Since that could be a friendship-ending mistake, he decided to cut his losses while she was still speaking to him. At least, he thought she was still talking to him. Considering they were both preoccupied trying to catch their breath, he couldn't be certain.

"Did we just…" Her voice trailed off as she took in another breath. He knew exactly where she was going with that question.

"Yep." His one-word answer seemed to entertain her, and her smile lit up her entire face. It was one of the things he'd always loved about her. That easy smile and the effect it had on him. Every time she brought it out, the world seemed a little more colorful, a little bit brighter and whole lot better on every front.

Rather than get too caught up in why his heart just flipped when she locked gazes with him, he chuckled to himself before retrieving Red's leash. Normally, the golden retriever mix ran free, but he was about to take her to the crime scene and he wanted to be able to keep her from roaming as they investigated.

The law had performed their own investigation earlier and Declan wanted to be able to take a look at what they might have seen. He'd have to rely on their expertise for fingerprints, if any had been collected, and gunpowder residue testing.

"Let's head back to the B&B," he said after holding Red's leash. All he had to do was rattle it around in his hand for his dog to charge toward him, stopping at his side. Looking at her caused nothing but happiness, and also reminded him of the worst in people. He still couldn't fathom the cruelty it took to dump a sweet girl like her on the side of the road still attached to her crate. No water. No food. His fingers tightened around the leather strap just thinking about it.

There had to be a special place in hell for anyone who could be cruel to such a sweet creature. He hoped Red had been young enough to forget the entire incident. She'd been trusting as all get-out from the minute he found her. Although, he couldn't for the life of him figure out why she would be. It was just her nature. Being that young had probably been a good thing for her, and he must've found her pretty quick after the dump. He was grateful for whatever stopped her from being damaged for life. For not being able to trust humans. He patted her on the head as he thought about the life she lived now. She was spoiled beyond belief and would be every day for the rest of her life just *like she deserved. To say she held a special place in his heart was a lot like saying apples were a main ingredient in apple pies.*

Piper trailed behind a couple of steps as they exited the barn. Her mood shifted and he hoped like hell she wasn't regretting the kiss. Personally, it ranked right up there with the best he'd ever experienced.

"Everything okay?" He stopped at the doors.

"Yes. I guess." There was something very not okay about the sound of her voice right then.

He'd ask if he was the problem, but he wasn't sure he wanted to know the answer to that question. Instead, he settled on, "Do you want to talk about it?"

She heaved a sigh. "Being here makes me happy, Declan. I have so many happy memories of this ranch." She paused long enough to bite down on her bottom lip before continuing. "Like, remember all those times we played hide and seek or tag right here in this barn and backyard?"

He chuckled at the memories. "I hadn't thought about it much lately. I get my blinders on and all I think about is what has to be done on the small stretch of track in front of me. Like checking and repairing fences or tagging calves. Now that you mention it, we had a lot of good times out here, didn't we?"

"Some of the happiest times of my life. This place represents so much more to me than a family home. It's

my childhood," she said, and he could hear emotion straining her voice.

He could see where she'd had to grow up during and after her father's trial. Declan hated it even more that she'd had to move away. He never really knew how she was doing or if she was handling her new life okay. She had a lot of change right before high school—a time when consistency was important because the most internal growth seemed to happen during those years. Having a strong base had gotten him through those rocky times.

He'd lost his best friend and that had been bad enough. He couldn't imagine going through that alone, which was exactly what she'd done.

"Do you want to stick around for a little while? We could stay here for the night. Head back in the morning," he offered.

"I wish. Gran needs me, so I probably should get back. I'm worried about her, Declan."

"I know." He'd seen the memory lapse and the agitation earlier. "We'll get her the help she needs. Her doctor should be able to get more resources to help with in-home care and help ease your load. Between running her business and taking on Owen's job, you'll need extra hands around."

She shot a look at him that he didn't immediately catch the meaning of. And then it dawned on him.

"I said we and I meant it. I'm here now. I care about your family and I want to be part of the solution. You don't have to do this alone, Piper." His words were meant to be reassuring but she ducked her head and refused to look up at him.

"Thank you, Declan." Her words were quiet. There wasn't a whole lot of conviction in them. She crossed her arms over her chest, like she'd just closed herself off to him.

So, he pulled her against his chest and wrapped his arms around her. "We'll figure it out, Piper."

"I can't go to prison. She'd be all alone." Those words, barely spoken out loud, were knives to his chest.

"No, she won't. And you won't."

"You can't promise me that. A man most likely died from my shotgun." Her body trembled and her voice shook.

"Let's not get ahead of ourselves," he soothed. "Let's take it one day at a time. And if that's too much to think about, we'll take it one hour at a time. If an hour is too much, we'll take it one minute at a time."

It had always helped him to slow down his thinking when life got too far ahead of him.

He felt her nodding against his chest and figured he'd take the progress. If she'd let him in, he would help her get through this. That was a big if. Piper wasn't the type to open up. He'd been her best friend and it had been all too easy to walk away from him and deal with life on her own. Her survival instinct of closing the ranks and shutting everyone out made for a lonely life.

When he really thought about it, she'd always gone dark when life got to be too much. She'd get quiet and sometimes disappear for a day or two. Maybe he could get her to open up a little bit and talk about what was going on inside her head.

"Hey," he started but she took a step away from him before he could finish.

"We should get back if you want to stop by the site." She walked toward the parking lot.

Declan looked at Red, who stared up at him like she didn't know what to do, either. He shrugged. Clearly, he was no good at breaking down Piper's walls. But he could be there for her. At the very least, she needed to know that he had no plans to abandon her now that she was home.

He was there for as long as she needed him or until she told him to leave.

"YOU CAN DROP me off at the front," Piper said to Declan on the drive home. Home? What was that anymore?

The ranch had been the closest thing, but shouldn't that honor be reserved for the B&B? For Gran?

Piper stared out the passenger window, unable and unwilling to go there with Declan. He was being kind, and she knew on some level that he meant every word of wanting to be by her side during this difficult time. Then what?

Or, worse yet, what if she did end up going to prison? She didn't murder Mr. Whitaker but experience had taught her that innocent people sometimes went to jail. There were wrongful convictions. It happened. It had happened.

Maybe her family was cursed with sheer bad luck. And, no, she didn't want to believe that. Yet, she couldn't ignore the facts. Her father had been wrongly convicted. Bad luck. Her Gran, who was the kindest and loveliest person ever to walk the earth, was losing her memory. Bad luck. And, now, all appearances said Piper was being set up for a murder charge. Bad luck.

Okay, the last one felt a lot more like being conspired against, but why her? Bad luck, an annoying voice in the back of her head reminded.

Piper had given up a job she loved…well…if not loved then one she was good at. She made enough money to rent an apartment in downtown Austin and drive a decent car. She was independent, both financially and in the relationship department. She took care of herself, and that always boosted her confidence. Independence was a good thing.

"Did you really mean that?" Declan's low hum cut into her heavy thoughts.

"What?" She had to think for a second. "Oh. The part about dropping me off instead of taking me to the site?"

"Yes." That one word was spoken so curtly that it took her back. She glanced over and saw how intensely he stared at the road ahead.

Red was seated in the second row of the dual cab pickup. Even she perked up at the sound of her master's voice.

"I just thought you might want to see it for your—"

"Well, I don't." He cut her off.

The rest of the drive was spent in silence. There was something simmering between them and she realized it was probably her fault. Declan had been going out of his way to offer his friendship and she realized that she must've hurt him. Then, there was the moment between them in the barn, a kiss so intense it had scrambled her brain.

She was really bad with intimate relationships and forget close friendships. He could ask pretty much anyone in her office where she'd been dubbed ice queen. Oh, no one ever called her that to her face. It was always behind her back or in quiet hallway chatter. She'd heard the whispers a few times after leaving a conference room where no one expected her to be.

Did it hurt?

She'd be lying if she didn't admit that it bothered her. She also couldn't deny the fact that she had a well-developed ability to shut down her emotions. Her boss had said she was the least 'complicated' person who'd ever worked for him.

Piper put in her time, did an excellent job at pretty much everything by his account, and demanded nothing of him in return except a paycheck and annual raise.

He'd called her a dream employee and said he would miss her once she was gone. Despite being married, he'd also made it abundantly clear that he was 'available' if she ever needed anything or anyone to talk to. Ick. And when she'd handed in her notice and told him the reason, he'd gone into a spiel about how his own mother had lost her memory and the toll it had taken on him. She would've felt sorry for him except that she realized his mother was still very much alive and well. He'd made a sympathy play.

Piper had shut off her emotions after walking out the door. She'd convinced herself she was happy not to be working for a lying jerk anymore. Maybe he'd seen weakness when she'd almost cried while turning in her letter of resignation and decided to use the opportunity to pounce.

After this morning and hearing Red's story, she was losing her confidence in humanity. Right up until she glanced to her left and saw Declan. He was a very large part of the tiny amount of good left in her world. And she'd just offended him.

Nice one, Piper.

She was really crushing it today. The excuse that she'd been through the wringer might be true, but it was just that. An excuse. Declan deserved more than her looking for an escape hatch.

Piper was beginning to realize just how bad she'd gotten about being someone's friend. To be fair, it had been a while. She'd been close with her father. And, of course, with her gran. But that wasn't quite the same as letting someone in.

There was Lisa at the office, her mind tried to argue. Yeah. Lisa. Piper had gone out to lunch with the woman three times in two years. No one would call that a friendship even though Piper enjoyed the lunches and even the conversation.

She conceded to being more the stay-at-home-on-Friday-nights type, preferring a good book or new craft to work on to physical company. Friendships took an investment of time. Up until her father had died, she'd been busy caring for him. There'd been a few boyfriends over the years. None of whom she ever thought would cause the end of the world if she didn't speak to again. Not like the pain she'd felt when she'd lost Declan. That had been almost crippling. And yet, she'd found a way to tuck it away deep inside because her father had needed her. Their family unit, small as it might have been, was together and she didn't want to do anything to remind him of the past.

The realization was a punch to the solar plexus. It made it hard to breathe. She felt wobbly and a little bit out of control. The feeling was a little too familiar. The tightness in her chest. The difficulty breathing. The dark cloud hanging over her head.

Breathe. She reminded herself, trying to talk herself through the panic attack. These had come on after her father's sentence. They were stealthy and gave no warning. They were like thieves, robbing her of any sense of lightness or joy.

Breathe. She planted herself in her surroundings. She was in Declan's truck, sitting next to her best friend. They were on the road, heading toward Gran's house.

Breathe. She reminded herself the feelings were real but on steroids. She was safe, despite feeling like the walls were about to cave in. She was doing better than it felt like in the moment. This feeling would go away, just like always. She could make it disappear faster by grounding herself in reality. Her brain was playing a trick on her.

She smoothed her fingers along the cloth strap on the seatbelt, taking in a few calming breaths. She looked over at Declan.

He was there and he was real.

10

Declan leashed Red after parking at the B&B.

The wall that had come up between him and Piper was frustrating. He could acknowledge that the kiss was probably a bad idea despite the fact his brain wanted to argue the opposite. Hard.

They'd gotten swept up in the moment—and it was one he'd remember for a long time. But they'd crossed a line of friendship that probably shouldn't be breached. They'd pushed a boundary that made it difficult to come back from, especially because his mind kept circling back to the electric current that tethered them and the power in one kiss that had him wishing for more. A lot more.

Normally, Declan didn't do more in a relationship. He dated. He enjoyed his freedom. He had great sex. And now one kiss had him rethinking everything he thought he knew about hot sex. Without a doubt, sex with Piper would blow his mind. It would bring physical contact to a whole new level.

Couldn't exactly say he was ready to redefine his entire viewpoint on the matter.

Those were the thoughts rolling around in his mind when he hopped out of the driver's seat and then circled the front of the truck to open Piper's door. She beat him to the punch, and he wondered if half the reason she was so eager to step away from the vehicle was so she could keep a safe physical distance between them. Not because she believed he would ever do anything to hurt her. There was no way on earth he'd raise a hand to her. But the fire simmering between them could erupt into an uncontrollable blaze.

She walked a few feet ahead toward the barn. He and Red gave her plenty of space. It seemed to be what Piper needed as the three of them walked beyond the barn and into the woods.

Knowing his former best friend, she needed to know he was there for her but didn't need him too close. He remembered the time she failed a history test by one point because she mixed up the date and studied for chemistry instead. She'd gone inside herself for two solid days over that one, wanting him nearby but not to talk. It was just her way. She'd always been hard on herself, holding herself to an almost impossibly high standard.

That same standard didn't apply to others. She was always ready and willing to offer compassion to anyone else for a slipup.

Judging from the way her shoulders hunched forward and she hugged her arms across her chest, she was bracing herself for being back on the scene. Every muscle in Declan's body urged him to reach out to her, put an arm around her, be her comfort.

Knowing Piper, unsolicited physical contact when she was in this mood would cause her to retreat like a tortoise in a shell. Definitely not the right play.

As the trees thinned, she dropped back until she was side by side with him and Red. Red, by the way, was enthusiastic on this walk. She saw this as an adventure in the woods right up until Piper stopped. She held out an arm, stopping Declan, too.

"Talk to me, Declan, or I can't keep going." Her words came out in between burst-like breaths.

"It'll be dinner time before we know it. I can order pizza from the place you like in town," he began.

A half smile ghosted her lips. "It's still there?"

"Haven't you been downtown since you've been back?" He was more than a little shocked at her response.

"Not really. I've only been here four days. Some homecoming," she said the last part low and under her breath.

"It's been a while since the last time I was there, but, as I remember the pizza with a garden on top was your favorite," he said.

"That shredded chicken is to die for." She seemed to catch those last words a little too late to reel them in.

"Who would think spinach and goat cheese with shredded chicken on top would make for a pizza?" he teased, liking the fact she seemed to relax around him again. It hadn't reached pre-kiss levels, but this was the first sign of hope they could get back there.

"I know, right." She reached out to him, grabbing hold of his arm. He ignored the heat that came from contact.

His thoughts shot to that kiss and how incredible her lips had felt as they moved against his. Her taste, the tea mixed with sweet honey that was uniquely Piper.

And since that was about as productive as walking a tightrope to cross a canyon, he forced his thoughts to the present.

"And how do they make that crust taste so good?" he continued with the pizza talk.

"It's insane." There was no joy in her voice like a few seconds ago but there was no fear, either. He'd take that as a win.

"I heard they have craft root beer now."

"That's even better," she said. "So you've brought up all these pizza memories, but is it even still on the menu?"

"I'm not sure. But we can ask," he offered. Part of the reason he'd stopped going to DOUGH was because it reminded him too much of her. Being around her again made him realize just how much that was true. It had been easy to keep those feelings tucked away in a place he never visited.

"I can almost smell it now," she said, wrinkling her nose in the most adorable way. It made him notice her full, pink lips. Bad idea.

Declan scanned the area as they broke through the tree line. He wanted to make sure the person responsible for the murder hadn't decided to return to the scene and, besides, he needed to refocus. Red was busy sniffing the ground and wagging her tail as she moved around beside him.

Birds flew out of the canopy.

"There's our boat," Piper declared, pointing to the shoreline of the lake. The boat looked like it was tied off somewhere as it bobbed in the waves. It wasn't there before so the deputy must've retrieved it.

They walked toward it, careful not to walk on any footprints that could be evidence.

"This is ours," she stated again after closer inspection. The two-man fishing boat was tied to a post that jutted out of the water.

Declan would need to wade into the water waist deep to be able to get a peek inside.

"Hold on." He handed over Red's leash and his phone, but she followed him anyway as he trekked out to get a glimpse. He'd been right about the waist-deep part. Red had stopped halfway out. She'd never been one to get in water over her head even though running along a shore was right up there with chewing on a bone.

"What do you see?" Piper asked.

"Blood." Light red water swished around at the bottom of the boat. There wasn't much else. "I'm guessing the deputy dusted for prints, but I have no idea how the water would come into play. At the very least, he can get a blood type to see if it matches the victim's."

A match could prove he was brought to this side of the lake by boat. It would also go a long way toward proving Piper's innocence because it fell in line with her statement.

She needed the win.

PIPER HAD TOLD the sheriff about a boat motor. This finding gave her a little bit of hope that her story could be corroborated.

126

A good investigator followed the evidence. Sheriff Justice struck Piper as someone who was good at her job. And yet, the dark cloud that had parked itself over Piper's head this morning was still docked there.

Bad news always came in threes. Piper's father had died. Her gran was losing her memory. And, now, Piper was under investigation for murder. Sounded about right for the way life had been treating her family.

She blew out a breath and studied the shoreline, walking until she found a trail. "Declan."

"Coming." True to his word, he was by her side in a couple of seconds. Soaked from the waist down and, in true Declan stride, not complaining about it no matter how uncomfortable he must be now.

Red was wet, too. Gran would have a heart attack when Piper brought her inside the house. At least, she hoped Declan planned to stick around.

The kiss they'd shared forced its way into her thoughts. She could scarcely fathom the heat in that one kiss. She knew one thing was certain, and maybe it was a sad fact about her life, but she'd never experienced anything like it in the past. There'd never been so much excitement and energy, so much sizzle and promise in one kiss her entire life.

Was that sad?

Maybe. Or, maybe it was just that good. Come on, it was Declan. The man was hotness on a stick. A physical attraction the size of a mountain wasn't in question. Of course she was physically attracted to him. Even in middle school he'd been the best-looking boy in school, and he was so much more than that to her. They had connected on such a deeper level. The question wasn't, why was she attracted to him? It was why was she ruining their friendship by acting on it?

Age was supposed to bring wisdom. Since Piper could count on one hand the number of friends she had, especially in town, it was more than stupid to make a mistake like that with him.

This was Declan, for heaven's sake. The guy who knew all her secrets in middle school. Well, not all of them. She'd kept the one about having a severe crush on him to herself. No diary writing on that one. No writing their names inside a heart on her notebook.

She couldn't risk it then and she couldn't risk it now.

Thinking about their relationship rather than the daunting task of facing the spot she'd found Mr. Whitaker was a defense mechanism. At least, that's what she tried to convince herself as warmth shot through her when his shoulder grazed hers.

So, basically, she was doing a great job of keeping her feelings in check.

Declan pressed his shoe into the earth beside a footprint. He bounced on that one foot a couple of times before stepping back.

"I'm a big guy, and yet my shoe didn't make nearly the same impression as that one," he said about the one leading up to the spot she'd found Mr. Whitaker.

"Which makes me think this person was carrying something very heavy." She stared at the prints.

"Someone is more likely."

She nodded as they followed the track to right where she found the body. No surprises there.

"The sheriff can't think I'd be able to carry Harry Whitaker by myself. I'm not exactly a weakling but he's six foot tall and weighs...what would you guess?"

"A hundred and seventy-five pounds, give or take," he estimated.

"That's more than I can handle."

"There's only one set of tracks, so he didn't have help," Declan agreed. "And I don't see any wheel marks, so he couldn't have used a wheelbarrow, either."

"Nope. The person who carried Mr. Whitaker had to have been strong," she reasoned. A tiny bit of hope blossomed in her chest at the findings.

"I'm guessing the killer is male based on the shoe imprint," he said.

"The sheriff's office has to have found all this, too." She sucked in a burst of air as more hope filled her chest. "She has my clothes and the shoes I had on. It's obvious the impression didn't come from me and there's no second set."

"Maybe they'll get a fingerprint on the boat. The shotgun was most likely wiped clean, but you never know. The killer could have been in a hurry and had to ditch the gun. You might have surprised him, and I'm still guessing it was a him at this point. I can't think of any women in Cattle Cove who are strong enough to single-handedly carry Mr. Whitaker of their own accord all the way over here from the boat."

She nodded, thinking along the same lines. "This is the first good news I've had so far today." Her statement seemed to put him off. She knew better than to question it.

Declan walked around with Red, surveying the area. He studied trees, mumbling something about checking to see if any of the branches had been broken off. She couldn't help thinking that he would've made a great investigator.

Declan fished his cell phone out of his pocket thankful he'd spent the extra money on the waterproof kind and took a picture of one of the impressions.

She hugged her arms to her chest, trying to stave off the slow tremors rocking her body. And then she turned her anxiety into anger. Life seemed to be throwing punch after punch and she was done letting it knock her down. She was ready to fight back, and her toughness kicked into high gear. The alternative was to worry herself sick and give into a system that hadn't protected her father. One that had taken too much.

Was this an all-around awful situation? That was a hard yes.

Was she going to let it destroy her? That was a hard no.

She'd been stuffing her feelings deep down long enough. Her dad was gone. Her beautiful gran was losing her vitality and sharp mind. And Piper was looking at possibly having to defend herself for murder.

The evidence she could see should clear her. But since she trusted law enforcement about as much as an ex-con, she would make her own case.

"What else do you see?" she asked Declan. Having him on her side might just be the best part of all this craziness, of life's craziness.

Feeling the fight in her rise like a steady morning sun, she exhaled.

"No branches were broken, so the person who brought Mr. Whitaker here probably left the same way he came," Declan said.

She searched around on the ground for more shoe prints, this time heading back toward the lake.

"There's nothing heading back toward the water."

"I'm not surprised. You said the boat wasn't there earlier. You would've noticed your own vessel," he surmised.

"And I heard the motor," she reminded him.

He nodded. "Your story matches everything I'm seeing here. The deputy has to have seen all this, too."

"How old is James Bowker?" she asked.

"Around your dad's age, I'd guess." It seemed to dawn on him why she'd ask. "He has two sons and a daughter. One of them might be strong enough."

From everything she knew about criminal cases, a murder weapon belonging to her wasn't exactly a good sign.

The thought her future could hinge on a whether or not a deputy did his job well wasn't exactly comforting.

11

T he sun had started its descent. Being in the

woods made it dark earlier. Declan had seen everything he came for. Based on his observations so far, there was no possible way Piper could be considered a suspect. The murder weapon belonging to her was a problem, but it seemed to him the gun was most likely stolen. Probably wiped clean and ditched. He fully expected to learn there were no prints on the weapon.

With his statement on his time of arrival, combined with hers, the stories meshed. Not that knowing any of this was probably much of a comfort to Piper given her history.

A quick glance at her as she stared at the spot where she'd tried to revive Mr. Whitaker said she needed to go. Based on the stress lines of her frown, the sooner the better.

Plus, his jeans were literally sticking to his legs after going into the water. He'd finished taking pictures using his camera phone and had gathered enough evidence to back up her story should the deputy somehow 'lose' what he'd taken.

Declan had seen the justice system work for his family, but he wouldn't leave anything to chance when it came to Piper. He moved beside her and Red was at his side.

"There's no way a person carried the victim all the way here before taking off in a hurry and didn't leave behind some DNA," he reassured. "Sheriff Justice and her deputy will find it. She has come through for my family countless times already."

"I hope you're right," she said. The weariness to her voice told him how little energy she had left. It had been a day for the books.

The trio turned toward the house and backtracked until they made it to the back porch.

"I'm not dripping anymore, but I doubt your gran will want me traipsing through the house like this. I have a spare gym bag in my truck with enough supplies to get through a couple of days," he said as she shot him a look. When her eyebrow raised, he caught on.

"Do you frequently have overnight trips?" she asked, and he detected a hint of jealousy in her tone. Under different circumstances, he would enjoy it. Nothing about this situation made him want to smile.

"No." Even though the day's events had been awful, he couldn't help but think how good it was to see Piper again. The thought of picking up their friendship where they'd left off was a bright spot in thick gray clouds.

An annoying voice in the back of his mind picked that moment to remind him that he didn't normally go around kissing his friends. He almost cracked a smile. There'd been no 'friendly' kisses with the kind of passion that heated his blood at first touch. He'd never gone from friendly peck on the cheek to ready to rip clothes off and bury himself inside someone before. So, yeah, he was swimming in uncharted waters.

"Never mind." She shook her head. "You didn't have to answer that because it's none of my business."

"We're friends, aren't we?" He tried to hide the blow to the chest that came with her statement. It had rolled off her tongue so easily, so naturally that he almost forgot how quickly she'd gone from innocent kiss to mind-blowing in a matter of seconds.

"I hope so. Because I can really use one right now, Declan."

Point taken. They both knew that anything else would just confuse the situation.

"That kiss was a bad idea," she continued before blinking up at him. "No matter how hard I try to push it from my mind, I can't."

Didn't those words turn up the heat outside in the snap of a finger.

"Yes," he agreed. "It was."

"I'm glad you think so, too," she said but there was no conviction in those words. And none in her eyes, either, when she locked gazes. "So, don't get the wrong idea…"

She pushed up to her tiptoes and kissed him. He should probably stop her. He should probably pull back instead of swallow her little moan of pleasure. He should probably be the voice of reason in a near-boiling-point situation.

And since that didn't work out so well for him, he decided to go all-in. He looped his arms around her waist as her body pressed flush with his.

Red tugged at her leash at about the same moment the hairs on the back of his neck prickled.

Declan gathered himself enough to stop the momentum—momentum that was propelling them into those uncharted waters at a breakneck pace. He glanced around and saw a male figure inside the kitchen.

"Are you expecting company?" he asked Piper, who was still in that momentary fog of desire that was threatening to overwhelm him as well.

She shook her head like she was trying to shake it off. Taking a step back seemed to help. "No." Panic filled her gaze. "The sheriff?"

"Not exactly. I can't tell from here, but I didn't see the guy in the kitchen window wearing a uniform."

"What guy?"

Declan crossed the window again after a few seconds.

"That one," Declan pointed out.

Piper gasped. She brought her hand up to cover her mouth. "No. That doesn't seem right."

"A guest?"

"There was no one on the books for today," she admitted. "Business has been slow lately."

"I can change my pants later." He clasped their fingers and was already heading toward the back door. Red seemed to read his mood because her hackles raised, and she started a low-throaty growl.

"It's okay, girl," he soothed.

Red was at a solid jog beside them as they hopped up on the back porch. Declan stopped long enough to toe off his boots and Piper did the same with hers. His water-logged socks came off next.

"Gran," she called out as soon as he opened the door.

"In here," Gran said, and he could feel the muscles in Piper's hand tense up.

"She's safe," he whispered so only she could hear.

"Safe isn't a word I'm all that accustomed to, Declan."

137

"That's about to change if I have anything to say about it," he admitted.

"WHAT'S GOING ON IN HERE?" Piper asked, eyeing the massive man's back. She could've sworn Declan sneered when the guy turned to face them.

"You must be Brody Axel," Declan offered a handshake.

Brody took it. The tension in the room ratcheted up a few notches.

"Nothing is happening, sweetie." Gran drew her eyebrows together and pursed her lips. "What do you think is happening?"

There was something in Brody's left hand that she couldn't quite see. Tucked behind his back, he was shielding it from view. Didn't that send warning flares sky high. Brody took a couple of strategic steps backward before looking Declan up and down as he reclaimed her hand. Brody's gaze lingered a few seconds longer than she was comfortable at their linked fingers. Instinct made her want to jerk her hand away, but Declan's grip tightened.

"Your gran thought it would be a good idea if I stopped by tonight," Brody said. She'd only seen him from a distance before. He was huge up close. Not quite as big as Declan but he came in a close second. He had jet black hair that was tight cut, like he was ex-military. His black eyes were intense and when they perused her one word came to mind, wolf. He was thick. Thick arms. Thick neck. Thick body.

He was big in a way that was intimidating but that might just be the way he carried himself. Shoulders forward, chest puffed out, like he was ready for a fight. And she wasn't sure if Declan gave it much thought or it was just plain protective instinct that had him positioning himself in between her and Brody.

His face was hard and looked like he hadn't smiled in years. There were slash marks in his forehead and hard lines around his mouth. The word, intense, came to mind when thinking about how to describe him. And dark.

Brody had tattoos up both of his arms. Sleeves, she believed they were called. And one on the back of his left hand. He was holding something that had been rolled up, hiding it from view.

"She did?" was all Piper could say. It wasn't really a question.

"Yeah, but since this seems like a bad time." He started backing away. "And you already have company. I'll come back another day."

"You can stay for supper," Gran insisted.

"No, he can't. We already have company, Gran. I'm sorry that I forgot to tell you earlier." There was no way she was going to let Declan be made uncomfortable after everything he'd done for her today, was still doing.

"Oh, well, I suppose…"

Gran didn't need to finish her sentence with the speed in which Brody was backing out of the room.

"I'll stop by another time," he said and before anyone could argue or tell him not to bother, he'd turned and was out the front door.

"You don't have to fix me up with anyone, Gran." Piper mustered the kindest voice she could under the stressful circumstances of the day. She squeezed Declan's hand, hoping for support. "Declan and I are more than just friends."

He let go of her hand and her heart dropped. Was he going to blow her cover? Piper didn't want to mislead her gran. In fact, it felt pretty awful. But she also didn't want the woman finding another guy to 'show up' for dinner. Or coffee. Or anything else that insinuated a date. Piper might not have been very good at finding someone she wanted to spend the rest of her life with but that didn't mean she needed someone to step in and do it for her.

She flexed her fingers a couple of times, ready to defend herself when Declan made a move. He wrapped his arm around her shoulders and gave her a kiss.

Gran's face turned as red as a hot burner. Her eyes lit up.

"I knew the two of you would make a perfect couple," she exclaimed. "I should get busy. Dinner is—"

"On me tonight," Declan said. "How about pizza?"

Gran's eyes lit up and she clapped. "That'd be just fine."

Forget the fact pizza wasn't her grandmother's favorite. She liked it okay, but she rarely ever ate more than one piece on the rare occasion Piper had ordered it. Did Gran remember her food preferences?

"I need a quick change of clothes and I'll be right down." He disappeared up the back staircase with Red on his heels.

Gran looked at Piper. "Dear, you look tired. Are you all right?"

"I'm fine." She wanted to add, all things considered. "How about you? You've been going all day. Did you get your nap earlier?"

141

Gran shook her head. "Too much excitement going on with your dad's trial coming up."

"That already happened," Piper said.

"It did?" Gran got flustered again. She snapped her fingers. "Oh, that's right. I remember now."

Piper had no idea if she was supposed to correct her Gran during these memory lapses or not. Being here for a few short days, she didn't have a good handle on how to proceed. She would, though. She'd find the best specialist and ensure Gran received the utmost care. Piper would educate herself on the disease, so she would be able to provide the best care.

The crazy part was that so much of the time Gran seemed fine. It was so easy to slip into thinking that everything was really okay. Gran remembered so much from when Piper was young. Her memory was ironclad there. It seemed to be the more recent events that Gran had the most difficult time hanging onto.

"Well," she exclaimed. "I better get started making dinner."

"Declan decided to order pizza. Doesn't that sound like fun?" With every slip, Piper's heart fisted in her chest and a little bit more of Gran seemed out of reach.

"What a great idea," Gran stated. Maybe it was the stressful events of the day that had sent her into the memory loop. This day definitely fell into the category of bad day.

Declan descended the stairs with Red by his side. "I called ahead, and food will be ready by the time we get there."

"Will you be okay, Gran?" Piper didn't feel good about leaving her gran alone on such a bad day. She also realized that she wouldn't be able to stay by Gran's side twenty-four-seven. She needed to dig into the financials so she could see where they stood on hiring at least part-time help at COZI. And she needed to search for healthcare resources.

"On second thought, why don't you stay here with Red. I'll make a quick run." Declan's offer was just the out Piper needed.

"I think that's a good idea," Piper said. She turned to Gran as he took off out the back door. "Do you want to play cards?"

"Maybe after I make dinner," Gran repeated herself from a few minutes ago.

"Pizza has already been ordered," Piper gently reminded.

"Oh, that's wonderful." Gran threw her hands up in the air. "Then, I guess I have time for a hand."

"How about Uno?" Piper asked, hoping the name would ring a bell. They used to play together all the time when Piper was a kid. Since Gran's long-term memory seemed to be in better shape than her short-term memory, she decided to give it a go.

"My favorite." Gran clapped again and smiled.

"I'll get the deck." That little win caused Piper's heart to swell inside her chest. She'd take it. She'd take any moment she could get with Gran that felt like old times. She had questions for Gran about Brody's visit, but those would have to wait. She ran into to her bedroom and retrieved the deck from her nightstand, thinking about how many games they'd played in her bed before lights out.

Gran was hunting through the cupboard when Piper returned. Her stomach tightened at the thought of losing this small victory.

"What are you looking for?" she asked.

"Hold on just a minute. I think it's back here somewhere." She rooted around a little bit more. Then came, "Ah-hah. I knew it."

She pulled out a bag of jellybeans.

Now, Piper's heart really did sing. She wiped a stray tear. But it wasn't a tear of sadness. It was a tear of joy. Of remembering. Of the Gran she loved being with, mentally present. She'd take it.

With a smile that most likely ran ear-to-ear, she walked over to the table and took a seat. She opened the deck and dealt cards as Gran joined her.

"Gran, what did Brody want?" she asked after counting out seven cards each.

"He had a piece of paper that he needed my signature on. Said he was asking everyone in the area to sign a petition for something or other. I think it was for lights on the county road and he needed so many to have it considered."

Funny, he didn't ask for Piper's signature.

Or Declan's for that matter.

12

"Pizza is here." *Declan had to smell it the entire way back to COZI and his stomach wouldn't stop growling. He carried in the extra-large pie, stopping as soon as he got a look. Piper and her gran laughing and playing Uno in the kitchen was a sight for sore eyes.*

"I'll get plates." Piper stood up and then joined him at the counter.

Instinct had him wanting to reach over and give her a kiss, so he squashed that friendship-killing idea real quick.

A few minutes later, the three of them were eating and talking like the old friends they were. Red had been fed first and let out for a bathroom break. She was presently lying at Declan's feet.

The mewls of pleasure Piper released as she ate wasn't helping him keep her in the friendship zone.

"I was just talking to Gran about Brody's visit," Piper finally said.

"Oh yeah? What did he want?"

"Her signature on a petition." She said the last word a little slower and more carefully. "Right, Gran?"

"Something or other to do with lights on the county road," Gran confirmed. "I didn't bother reading it. I just signed where he told me to. I don't drive anymore but if it'll keep others safe."

"Sounds like something we all should sign." Declan glanced at Piper and saw the frown on her face. "Maybe we should stop by his place in the morning and ask to sign it, too."

"That's a great idea actually." Piper pursed her lips like she did when she was angry.

"I doubt I could eat another bite," Gran said, setting the crust on her plate. "Declan, thank you for dinner."

"My pleasure, ma'am."

"If you'll excuse me, I'm plumb tuckered out." Gran pushed to standing. "Oh, I almost forgot. We have a guest coming tomorrow. A family. I told them check-in is at three o'clock, but they're welcome to come any time."

"What are their names?" Piper asked.

"I wrote it down somewhere." Gran shrugged. "I'll give it to you in the morning."

Again, Piper frowned.

"I'll check the book in case you wrote it there," Piper said.

Gran smiled warmly and said, "Goodnight, princess."

Piper blushed as she stood up. She hugged her grandmother and it was about the sweetest thing Declan had seen all week.

The two of them were going to have a busy day tomorrow. That was, if Piper wanted him to stay over. He started cleaning up the dishes and they worked together putting away the leftover slices. There wasn't much. He refilled Red's water bowl, which she immediately emptied.

"Hey, Red. You want to go outside?" He glanced at the clock. It was later than he realized. Although, time had always flown when he was with Piper. There'd been countless nights he'd had to survive on four hours sleep because they stayed up way too late on the phone. He wasn't much of a talker except when it came to her.

Red's tail started working double time.

"All right, girl. Let's go." Declan walked over to the back door and let her out. He followed since they weren't exactly home and, as familiar as this place was to him, this was Red's first time there.

The back porch light was on and the barn was well-lit. Red darted across the yard and toward the barn.

"Hey, girl." He whistled at her, but she was locked onto something and had started barking at whatever was back there. Declan didn't like it, so he slipped into his still-wet boots and went after her.

"Red," he shouted as she broke through the tree line. Now, all his warning flares were firing. If there was a coyote she was chasing down or a wild hog, that wouldn't be good for her. The other possibility left a hole in his chest. The killer had returned.

He made a beeline for the trees as he shouted for Red again. She disappeared into the darkness and that sent his pulse racing.

"Red." Declan stopped and listened to get a direction. He heard a rustling noise and then she bounded out of the dark.

Chest heaving, tongue dragging, she practically bowled him over when he dropped down to her level. The thought of anything happening to her...

Declan couldn't go there. She'd been his loyal companion too long to consider the possibility of losing her. She was still young. He scratched her on top of the head before standing. As he turned toward the B&B, his heart gave a little flip.

There stood Piper on the porch, watching them. Chalk it up to nostalgia, but in that moment the world righted itself.

And since that line of thinking was about as productive as chasing a hot pepper with tequila, he shoved it out of his mind.

Red took care of business and the two of them jogged back to the house.

"She must've seen a rabbit or something." He left it at that. They both realized the implication that someone might have been out there watching the house. He saw it in Piper's eyes.

"I wasn't sure she was going to come back when you called her." Piper bent down and gave Red a good squeeze. Seeing those two together wasn't helping contain his feelings toward Piper. Friend zone. He repeated the words a couple of times, hoping they would stick this time.

"For a minute there, I thought the same thing." He didn't even want to think about anything happening to Red.

He followed Piper and his dog inside the house.

"I was thinking it might be a good idea for me to stay the night. There are plenty of open rooms here and—"

"Are you sure you don't mind?" she asked, and he was relieved that she seemed to want him to stay.

"Not one bit. In fact, I'd feel a lot better knowing the two of you are safe," he admitted.

She nodded, smiled and then feathered a kiss on his lips.

Friend zone.

"I need a shower." Preferably cold. He laughed at himself. One little kiss had never sent so much hot blood simmering through his veins.

"I'll just lock up and we can head upstairs," she smiled.

He waited as she secured the doors and cut off the lights. She double-checked windows and he realized how shaken up she was from the day, not that he could blame her.

Red jogged behind them as they cleared the stairs. It was late, coming up on ten o'clock. Ranchers started the day at four a.m. He used to joke they had the most in common with bakers and that it was true. They kept the same hours.

"I'll only be a few minutes." He motioned toward the bathroom as Red curled up next to the bed. He knew his way around having been here years ago.

"Take your time." An emotion flickered behind her eyes that he was keenly aware of. It looked a whole lot like need.

Again, not the image he wanted to take with him. But the one that, deep down, he needed.

THE LAST THING *Piper needed to do was watch a tiny bead of water as it rolled down Declan's chest. She'd showered down the hall, a benefit of living in a house with seven bedrooms and six baths, and was back in her room as he emerged from the shower.*

"I've been thinking about what you said earlier about your gran signing the document that Brody brought over." He looked good wearing nothing but pajama bottoms. She'd almost forgotten that was the way he slept, bottoms only. Her pulse kicked up a few notches now, though, and she had a hard time tearing her gaze away from his muscled chest.

"Oh yeah?" She tried not to attract attention to her flushed cheeks as she plopped down on the bed in her oversized T-shirt and boxers. Even her breathing was affected by Declan. The man was easy on the eyes with those ripples of muscles and what looked a heck of a lot like more than six-pack abs. Ranching did a body good.

"Have you considered asking her to sign over power of attorney?"

Piper blinked a few times to regain her bearings on the conversation. "Not really. But it is something I'm going to have to consider, isn't it?"

"It seems like a good idea considering your Gran's mental state. I was just thinking how easy it would be to get her to sign pretty much anything. She gets embarrassed and flustered when she realizes she's forgotten something. It wouldn't take much to throw her off track and trick her into signing a legal document."

"Like a 'petition?'" That one was still grinding on her. If Brody had been asking around about her, he could forget the possibility of a date. He wasn't her type and there was something about him that was off-putting. Something that caused her to watch what she said around him and keep her guard up.

"We definitely need to stop off by his place tomorrow morning and figure out what he got her to sign," he said.

She couldn't agree more. "Can you hit that light?"

"No problem."

"And, Declan?"

"Yes."

"Will you sleep in the bed alongside me like we used to?"

The look that passed behind his eyes made that feel like a dangerous question—but dangerous in the best *possible way. The best way to kill a friendship would be to take it to the next level.*

So, why did reminding herself of the fact seem futile?

"Sure." He hit the light and climbed in bed next to her.

She realized he didn't slide under the covers and that was probably for the best. It didn't stop her from scooting over next to him and then settling into the crook of his arm.

He wrapped his arm around her and feathered a kiss on her lips, just a light touch, before saying, "I'm here. You can sleep."

Piper dozed off in his arms, feeling more secure than she'd felt in years. And when a noise woke her, she immediately reached for Declan.

The noise, it turned out, was his cell phone.

"Sorry," he said. "I need to take this."

She sat up at the same time he did. The noise had alerted Red, who came around to Declan's side of the bed.

"Okay. All right." There was a pause, and the urgency in his voice sent her pulse racing. Her nerves were already on edge and this sounded like more bad news.

A glance at the clock said it was four a.m. to the dot. She couldn't explain the reason, but something told her to get up and get dressed.

"And you think it's real this time?" Declan's voice was guarded. She wished she could hear the other side of the conversation.

In the meantime, she raced into the bathroom, dressed and quickly brushed her teeth.

He ended the call as she re-entered the room.

"What is it? What's going on, Declan?"

"My dad. Fifteen minutes ago, he opened his eyes, and then asked for a cup of coffee." There was so much disbelief in his voice.

"And you don't think it's real?"

"We were tricked recently, but I want this to be true." He had that look on his face that warned not to get hopes up.

Hope wasn't a bad thing. In fact, sometimes it was all a person had to hang onto. It had gotten Piper through losing her father, twice. It was going to get her through caring for her gran. Not the hope of recovery but the hope Piper could give Gran the final years she deserved. He'd been right about the power of attorney last night. But, right now, she wanted to focus on his family.

"There's only one way to find out," she said to him.

Declan nodded, threw off the covers and hopped out of bed. She ignored the fact that waking up to him felt like the most 'right' thing she'd done since returning to Cattle Cove.

As he dressed, she had to face facts about her gran and move forward with her best interests in mind.

"I'll check on Gran and meet you downstairs," she said to Declan.

"I need to feed Red and take her outside. Think she'll be okay if I leave her here while we go to the hospital?" he asked.

"Gran would love that. I can leave her a note if she's still sleeping, which she should be. Think Red would mind being here?" She really was a great dog. Easy going. Piper was sickened at the thought anyone could do anything but love such a sweet animal.

"She's flexible. We take care of each other on the ranch and she likes to sleep in the barn sometimes. She's used to being around different people, not like my brother's dog. I'll tell you about Karma on the ride over." Declan was talking fast, which wasn't like him.

Unless he was on edge.

Learning that his father was awake clearly had him rattled. He'd been her legs yesterday when she was afraid she couldn't stand any longer. Today, it was her turn to support him.

"Are you sure you're okay to leave?" he asked, concern intensifying his dark eyes.

"I'm good, Declan. Yesterday was…hard for lack of a better word. You being here made all the difference. Now, it's my turn to be there for you."

"It's what friends are for," he said like it was no big deal. It was, though. It was a very big deal in her book.

"I'm starting to realize just how true that statement is. And that's why I want to be there for you today, Declan." She walked over to him and, without overthinking her next move, she wrapped her arms around his neck and gave him a kiss.

13

T he ride to the hospital had two qualities, speed and silence. Declan parked in record time. Piper was out of the passenger side before he could get around the front of the pickup.

The thought of another letdown loomed. Declan shoved it out of the way. There'd been so much certainty in Levi's voice. Declan decided to cling to the hope his father was not only waking up but would be fine. They could finally put this ordeal behind them and let the next phase of healing begin. They could find out once and for all if Uncle Donny contributed to their father's fall.

Scanning the lot, he recognized a few pickups. At least a few of his brothers were here. They must've just arrived, or he would have an update on his phone.

He reached for Piper's hand, linking their fingers as they rushed into the hospital's glass double doors with the word, EMERGENCY, written in red letters.

There was no need to stop and ask directions since he'd been there countless times in the past few months. He moved directly to the elevator bank that led to his father's floor, tapping the toe of his boot on the white sanitized tile while he waited to hear the 'ding.'

As soon as the doors opened, they moved inside. At this time of the morning, no one except nurses and doctors roamed the hallway. More of that toe-tapping happened in the elevator and as soon as the door opened, he bolted toward his father's suite. The only comfort came in the form of his link to Piper. Their physical connection kept him sane and grounded in a rare moment of vulnerability.

He issued a sharp sigh, locked gazes with Piper for a quick second and then opened the door to the suite. There was no one in the lounge area and the door to his father's room was propped open. Another strange thing happened. There was chatter and it sounded lively. Without another minute of hesitation, he beat feet to the next doorway.

Sure enough, his father was propped up, sipping coffee. A few of his brothers leaned up against the wall as the doctor scribbled notes on the chart. Levi stood closest to the door, but his back was turned to Declan.

His brother turned around and immediately pulled Declan into a hug. He broke contact with Piper, who seemed to shift behind him as though she needed protection from curious eyes. A.J. and his fiancée were there as well as Declan's slightly younger brother,

Jack. A couple of his cousins stood on the opposite wall, Reed and Cage.

"The others are on their way," Levi said, stepping aside to allow passage into the room. "The doctor says it's a miracle, but one he's seen before in a few rare cases."

"How is he?" Declan asked.

"As far as we know, he's alert and recovering." Levi looked as astonished as Declan felt. His brother's gaze shifted to behind Declan and onto Piper. He reached back for her hand, found it.

"You remember Piper," he said to Levi.

"It's really good to see you again," Levi said. If he was surprised, he didn't show it.

"You, too. It's been a long time." She smiled and bit her bottom lip.

"How's your grandmother?" Levi asked.

"She's up and down," Piper admitted, thanking him for asking. "I came back permanently to help her out over the next few years or however long she has. I want her to be able to live in her home. You know?"

Levi nodded. "It goes without saying, but if you ever need anything, don't hesitate to reach out. We're all here for you and your family."

"It means a lot to hear you say that, Levi."

"I'm serious. Any one of us is just a phone call or text away."

Declan appreciated the warm reception Piper received as the others chimed in, offering their support. If he didn't know better, he'd say Piper sniffed back a tear.

Before Declan could greet the others, the doctor turned toward Levi.

"How is he, Doc?" Levi asked.

"We never really know what's going to happen when someone wakes up from a coma after this amount of time passes. His vital signs are strong. He knows his name. He was confused about what day it was, but that's understandable considering how long he's been under. I expect in a few days that he'll be up and around." Doctor Gregory practically beamed. He'd been one of many doctors looking in on their father over the past few months. He had a personal friendship with their dad that went back long before Declan was a thought.

"Thank you, Doc," Levi spoke for the group, but it was A.J. who was at their dad's side before any of the others could get to him.

"I'll be back in an hour or so to check on him, but this is the best possible outcome we could've hoped for." Doctor Gregory patted Levi's arm. "Knowing your father, he'll be back working the ranch in a matter of days."

That was probably wishful thinking, but hope was a good thing in Declan's book. And this was the first sign of it with his father's case. This was the first time Declan could really breathe when it came to his dad. In fact, he heard a collective sigh of relief from his brothers and cousins.

"I'll call Miss Penny," Jack offered. "She's already on her way but there's no reason to make her wait for good news like this."

"How about our group text? Do you mind letting everyone know Dad's status?" Declan asked as his brother stepped into the lounge.

"Good idea." Jack gave a one-arm hug on his way out. He smiled at Piper, who responded with one of her own. Her smile was a reason to get out of bed every day.

Way to keep feelings in check, McGannon.

Declan shook that thought out of his head as he walked over to his dad's bedside.

"Doc Gregory said I took a spill in the equipment room," Dad had lost a little weight and his skin wasn't as tan as usual. His eyes didn't quite have their usual spark. But this was progress and Declan would take it.

"You don't know what happened to you?" Declan figured the question was worth asking.

Dad shook his head. There were so many questions about what happened when he took the fall that put him in this position. Others mounted about the half-brother who'd shown up recently after Uncle Donny made a call. The man liked to stir up the pot and no one believed Kurt Johnson, now McGannon, was family when he'd first shown up questioning his lineage. A DNA test confirmed that he was a McGannon even though his mother had never told him who his father was. He'd grown up without any idea his family was one of the wealthiest in Texas. The questions started mounting once they'd figured out that he was six months older than Levi. Levi had always taken great pride in being the oldest in the family. He'd welcomed Kurt with open arms after paternity was revealed, despite how much that had to sting. And then there was the issue of their dad's infidelity. He was obviously already married to their mother when he had an affair, which was also shocking. Clive McGannon had loved his wife to the point of never remarrying after she died.

So, it was confusing that he'd loved her to that level and yet seemingly had no problem having an affair.

Unanswered questions were stacking up. The biggest one, the one about whether or not Uncle Donny had aided in their father's fall, seemed like it would have to wait.

THE ROOM WAS LIVELY with chatter. Piper had forgotten how great it was to be part of something bigger. She couldn't even count the number of times she'd dreamed about being part of a large family. The fantasy included big dinners and Christmases spent around the fireplace roasting marshmallows and swapping stories. The smell of cinnamon and baked goods wafting through the house along with the pitter-patter of tiny feet.

The realization, the memory caught her off guard. There was a time when she'd wanted a big family of her own with lots of children, a happy and vibrant house.

Wow, she'd really blocked all that out in the past few years. She'd done a great job of cutting off those desires after her father's trial and conviction. Did she want those things now?

A small part of her tried to convince her that she did with the right person. It would take a special person to be able to put up with all that commotion, kids running through the house. And she didn't mean two-point-five with a minivan and a picket fence. She wanted like half a dozen.

For the first time in a long time, she smiled at the thought.

Kids.

Life had sent her down a different path. One that had her immersed in her work with room for little else. Much to her embarrassment, she'd even neglected Gran. To be fair, Piper didn't realize how badly her gran was declining. It had taken seeing her in person to drive home the point. Now, all she wanted to do was to help. Piper figured she'd be devoting the next few years to the woman who deserved everything good in life. A husband and kids were the last things she'd be able to focus on while caring for an aging relative. So, yeah, life was ironic. When she actually realized how much she wanted a husband and kids, the timing was so far off it wasn't funny.

Or maybe it was.

Then again, she was staring at a miracle. Mr. McGannon coming out of a coma after months was one for the books. A happy time for the family. A time to celebrate. A time to remember miracles sometimes happened.

Declan held onto her hand as he spoke to his father. The room was getting more crowded every few minutes and more smiling, welcoming faces filled her view. Miss Penny rushed in with Hawk on her heels.

After half an hour, Mr. McGannon declared that he wanted to stand up. A.J. and Jack were on either side of him, so they each took an arm. Miss Penny discreetly hit the nurse's call button. She was always on her toes, thinking about what was best for the man who had always seemed more family than employer.

A nurse scurried into the room and waved her arms in the air. "No, sir. We can't have you out of bed yet."

Mr. McGannon smiled in that easy way he always had. He looked down at his feet, which were firmly planted on the tile, and said, "It's a little late for that."

Not even his smile could cool down the steam rising from the nurse's body.

"Back to bed." Her voice said she meant those words. "And everyone out. He needs his rest."

"All due respect, ma'am, I've rested enough for one lifetime," Mr. McGannon said with a wink.

But, again, the nurse wasn't having it. "I'm sorry, but I'm afraid I have to ask you all to leave."

"If we can convince him to go back to bed, will you allow a few of us to stay in with him at a time?" Levi interceded.

The nurse folded her arms across her chest and issued a sharp breath. Mr. McGannon eased to sitting and A.J. replaced the blanket that had been draped over his father's legs.

"Does that pass muster?" Levi asked.

With a frown, she nodded. "Two in here at a time. No more than that. Everyone else needs to wait in the lounge area."

No one seemed ready to push the fiery nurse. The family filed into the next room, leaving the door open.

Miss Penny made her way over to where Piper stood next to Declan.

"I've been meaning to stop by and check on your grandmother. How is she?" Miss Penny brought Piper into a warm hug. There was something maternal about it that reached a place deep inside Piper.

"She has more good days than bad." She didn't add the words for now. The understanding look from Miss Penny made them unnecessary.

"I really need to stop by and see her more often. Will you be staying on?" Miss Penny's gaze shifted to Declan and back in a blink.

"She would like that. And yes, I'm here now. I'm planning to help run COZI from here on out."

"How wonderful that your grandmother has your support," Miss Penny said. "She's very lucky to have someone who loves her so much."

Those words, the sincerity in her eyes had Piper sniffing back the moisture gathering in her eyes. She couldn't afford to break down even though part of her wanted to do just that, to let the tears flow until there was nothing left. There were days when she wished she could cry and release all the pent-up anxiety and anger bottled up inside.

She'd never been a crier. Not since she was little. After her father's sentencing, she cried so hard she could barely breathe. And then, just like that, she decided never again. She made up her mind. After a while, it felt much less like a choice and more like the way she was built.

Miss Penny gave Piper another squeeze before moving onto Declan. She started to say something and then seemed to change her mind. Her eyes lit up like something had dawned on her. "You know who I ran into today?"

Declan shook his head even though it was a rhetorical question.

"James Bowker."

"Where was he?" Piper asked, not bothering to mask the shock and anger in her voice.

"At the post office. Looked like he was checking his P.O. box," she said.

"I didn't realize he kept one in town." Declan shot her a look. The timing of Harry Whitaker's death and James Bowker's sighting seemed like an awfully strange coincidence.

"Guess he does." Miss Penny shrugged. "Thought it was a little odd to see him after all these years."

"Thanks for letting us know." Declan fished his cell out of his front pocket. He pulled up the sheriff's contact and glanced at Piper.

A knock sounded behind them. They turned in time to see Sheriff Justice step inside the lounge.

"I was just about to call you," Declan said to her.

"You heard already?" the sheriff asked.

14

"**I**'m talking about James Bowker being spotted in town. Why do I feel like you're talking about something else?" Declan reached for Piper's hand, and some of his tension relaxed when he made contact.

"Because I am." She blinked, like she was expecting a fastball and was thrown a curve instead. "I'd like to tell everyone at once, if that's possible."

"A handful of us are here and some are still running the ranch," Declan said. "I can grab the others inside Dad's room."

Reed and Cage perked up. They'd been standing with Jack while Declan and Piper spoke to Miss Penny. Hawk never seemed to venture far from Miss Penny lately. He was standing close to her while keeping a low conversation with the others. Levi and A.J. were with Dad.

Declan let go of Piper's hand, leaving her there with the sheriff. He peeked his head inside his father's room. "Sheriff is here. She'd like a word with us."

Miss Penny was on Declan's heels. "I'll stay with your father while you boys hear what Laney has to say." Laney Justice had grown up in Cattle Cove and Miss Penny often slipped when referring to the sheriff she'd known since Laney was young.

Levi and A.J. immediately left their father's side and came into the lounge area with the others as Miss Penny and Hawk slipped in for a turn.

"I want to thank everyone for giving me the floor for a few minutes. It's important this next bit of news comes from me." Her gaze shifted to Reed and Cage, causing Declan's heart to fist. "Donny McGannon has been placed under arrest for attempted murder."

Reed stepped forward first as silence sat heavy in the room. The air became thick with tension.

"My uncle is awake. Why not go and ask him for yourself if my father tried to kill him?" Reed asked, his voice understandably heated and a little bit shocked. Declan couldn't say he was surprised since Donny's behavior had been shifty in recent months. The man liked to stir up trouble and it was no secret that he was angling for more control over the business his brother had built. The brothers had been handed a successful cattle ranch, but Declan's father had skyrocketed profits. Donny had cashed out and walked away from the family business years ago. His gambling habit and a healthy losing streak had caused him to return with his hand out, asking for more money. But in Declan's heart of hearts, he didn't want to believe that his uncle would be capable of attempted murder.

"I'm fully aware of what's going on in the next room and I hope your uncle gives us a contradictory statement. For now, I'm afraid that your father is in my lockup," Justice said.

"I'll pay his bond," Cage spoke up next.

Their cousins had to notice that none of Clive's sons made the same offer or volunteered to pitch in financially. Declan figured everyone had been avoiding drawing a line in the sand and taking sides on whether Donny was innocent or guilty.

Now?

There was a huge crack.

"That's up to a judge, Cage. I have no control over bail, if and when it's set," she informed.

"What do you mean if?" he asked.

"Again, that decision is up to the judge. If he views your father as a flight risk or a danger to himself or others, he can deny bail." Her words caused Reed to start pacing.

Reed was closer to Declan's father than to his own, but this news would rock anyone. Hell, Declan's father had stepped in as a father figure after Donny took off. So, Reed wasn't being disrespectful. He was concerned for Donny and, in his mind, he would see this as doing the right thing.

"We'll figure this out, Reed." Levi was the first to offer words of comfort.

In the middle of the chaos of the moment, their half-brother Kurt made his appearance. Of course that would happen now. Murphy's Law didn't disappoint. Anything that could go wrong was going wrong.

Then again, maybe that was the wrong way to look at it. Maybe Kurt's timing was perfect because the little girl sleeping on his arm quashed some of the tension mounting in the room. Reed excused himself and Cage followed. Levi didn't waste time going after them. Being the oldest, he'd always been the peacemaker and he always had a good sense of when to take a step back.

"That's my half-brother and his daughter," Declan said quietly to Piper. There was a spark in her eyes when she looked at Paisley that he'd never seen before. And it did things to his heart that were foreign, as well.

"Could I have a minute of your time," the sheriff interrupted the moment.

"Of course," Piper said, quickly refocusing her attention. She cleared her throat as they followed the sheriff into the hallway.

Outside of earshot, the sheriff stopped and then leaned against the wall. Declan took her relaxed posture as a good sign because the way this week was going, he had no idea what to expect.

He looped his arm around Piper's waist, and she leaned into him.

"What's on your mind, Sheriff?" he asked.

She looked to Piper. "This news probably won't be a surprise to you, but I thought you deserved to hear it from me. There were no fingerprints on your shotgun. They'd been wiped clean. And, the results of the gunpowder residue test showed trace amounts."

"Meaning?" She cocked her head to one side and her eyebrow came up.

"There wasn't enough residue on your hands for my department to conclude you fired a weapon," she clarified.

"Why would someone set me up?" She looked bewildered.

"It could've been a crime of opportunity," the sheriff said.

Declan shook his head. "If that was true, someone would've heard the shot. There are other, more efficient ways to kill someone than to come all the way over to COZI to take a shotgun."

The sheriff acknowledged his comment with a nod.

"I haven't been back for a solid week yet. There's no way I could've upset someone to the point they'd want to frame me for murder," Piper said.

"We need to look into what someone might have to gain for answers." The sheriff hit on the same point

Declan and Piper had come to yesterday afternoon. Motive.

Then again, maybe someone just wanted Harry dead and figured using Piper's weapon was easy. On second thought, it didn't seem reasonable considering the person would have had to do a lot of back and forth between properties.

Revenge topped his list. "James Bowker was seen in town."

"He testified against my father and was a big part of the reason my father went to prison," Piper supplied. "He said my father talked him into investing money in a scam that bankrupted him."

The sheriff nodded as she took out a notepad and jotted down the name. "Who saw him?"

"Miss Penny," Declan answered.

"Did she say where?"

"The Post Office. He was checking his P.O. box apparently," Declan continued as Piper nodded.

"I'll talk to Miss Penny about it. Thank you for letting me know," she said before looking directly at Piper again. "And there's no one else you know who might have a problem with you coming back to Cattle Cove?"

She blew out a sharp breath. "I wish I did."

PIPER WAS DEAD SERIOUS. She had no earthly idea who would set her up for murder. She'd never said an offensive word to a soul. It just wasn't in her nature.

"If anything changes about your situation or you remember anything important, I'd appreciate a call," the sheriff said.

Piper said she would, and she and Declan started to walk away from the sheriff. And then she remembered Brody's visit.

"Hey, Sheriff. What do you know about a petition for lights on the county road near Gran's place?" she asked.

"Nothing. I've never heard of it. Why?" The sheriff seemed genuinely caught off guard by the question. She looked to draw a blank.

"Our neighbor, Brody Axel, claimed he was collecting signatures. I never saw the petition, but he supposedly asked Gran to sign it." Then again, with Gran's memory, he could've asked for something completely different and she just forgot. She'd had a bad day yesterday and Piper figured it was from all the stress of learning a man, a neighbor, was killed on COZI property. Plus, the obvious fact that he was murdered with Piper's shotgun.

It was a lot to unpack for anyone. Speaking of which, she needed to get back to her gran's house.

"I'm not aware of any. I'll ask around at the office just in case," the sheriff said before entering the lounge, no doubt to ask Mr. McGannon a few questions about his brother.

"Do you need to stay here?" she asked Declan once the sheriff was out of earshot.

"You already heard the nurse. I'll make sure my family lets me know if anything changes. Right now, though, there's a long line of people who want to spend time with him," Declan said. "I'd be in the way if I stuck around."

Knowing his father would not only survive his 'accident' but would be able to walk again boosted his spirits and rightfully so. An unspoken burden had been lifted.

"Plus, we need to talk to Brody Axel. There's no way it's safe for you to go alone," he added and there was a hint of something in his voice—jealousy?

Why did that make her heart flip-flop? She told herself that hers and Declan's friendship had been special to her and it was nice to see that it was special to him, too.

This time, she reached for his hand and her heart did that flip-thing again when their skin made contact. When it came to Declan, she was losing the battle to contain her feelings. As much as she tried to convince herself being together this much was temporary, her heart wanted to argue for more. Her traitorous heart wanted her to believe there was more between them than friends. Granted, they'd shared a few mind-blowing, toe-curling kisses—kisses that made her believe in love again. The best way to ruin a good friendship was to let it become something else, something more. All her romantic relationships ended, usually not long after they started and usually because she knew when to cut bait.

It was probably just Gran's situation or maybe the fact that Piper had lost her father that had her feeling like she might be ready to at least think about getting serious with someone. She had to admit that looking at Declan's niece, that round angelic face, had tugged at her heart and made her ovaries cry.

Despite the sizzle in the kisses she and Declan had shared, getting involved with her best friend was the quickest way to end up friendless. A voice deep in the back of her mind called her out. Nothing with Declan felt temporary. And maybe that scared her even more.

Rather than looping the same argument in her head a dozen more times, she shifted gears to thinking how nice it was just to have Declan back in her life. To have someone who had her back for a change. To have someone she had history with who cared about her as much as she cared about him. Because, bottom line, they had a strong bond. One that she needed if she was going to get through what she hoped would be several years left with her gran.

"I still need to get through Gran's financial documents and see where she stands," she said, thinking out loud.

"You have a guest coming today. Other than that, does it seem like business has been good?" he asked.

"Not really. Nothing to speak of. I'm wondering how she's done as well as she has," she admitted.

Gran had never once asked for money or help for that matter. She'd always been fiercely independent.

"Why not sell COZI?" he asked. "It might be easier to focus on caring for your grandmother if you didn't have the day-to-day operations to think about. Plus, with Owen gone, you'll need to find a way to do his work. Have you been in contact with him?"

"No. He took off before I got home. His mother was in a bad way according to Gran," Piper said. "Do you know him very well?"

"Me? No. But, like I said before, I tend to mind my own business and stick to the ranch."

She already heard the whispers of the nurses, talking about how many McGannons were in the house. It must get old having a name that drew attention, especially for someone like Declan who had always been a private person.

"Does it drive you crazy sometimes?" she asked as they exited the hospital.

"What?"

"The chatter. I must've heard three nurses gasp when we walked past." She laughed.

"What's funny?"

"I forget sometimes that I'm walking around with a celebrity," she teased.

"Not you, too." He groaned like he was in physical pain.

"I mean it, Declan McGannon. You're a big shot around here."

"Oh yeah?" He tugged at her hand until he'd situated her in front of him, her back to his vehicle. "Does all this 'fame' win me any favors?"

Dangerous territory. Because her heart said he didn't need fame to win any favors from her. Logic tried to shut it down real quick but where was reason when it came to matters of the heart?

And when their gazes locked, straight up electricity zinged through her body, seeking an outlet.

He stared into her eyes for a long moment. So long, in fact, she almost asked him to kiss her again.

When his lips started lowering toward hers, warmth circled low in her belly. Anticipation mounted as her nerve endings hummed with unchecked electrical current.

She closed her eyes and thought about the tenderness of his lips despite his face of hard angles. His breath smelled like a mix of coffee with a hint of peppermint toothpaste. But Declan's scent was all spicy and masculine. It would be so easy to get lost right now.

Instead of claiming her lips like she wanted, no needed him to, he pressed his forehead against hers.

"You're a little too tempting. You know that?" His words came out low and gravelly. His voice raspy.

She could say the same thing about him. Instead of talking, she grabbed two fistfuls of his shirt, tugging him toward her.

"I thought you said kissing was a bad idea," he said against her mouth.

"Yeah? Because I think you're remembering that wrong. I think I said you kissing anyone but me is a bad idea."

He laughed, a low rumble in his chest.

"I can't keep going back and forth on this one, Piper." His chest heaved in rhythm with hers.

Damn, that he'd made a good point. It wasn't good for either one of their sanity no matter how incredible it felt in the moment. And it felt beyond anything she'd ever experienced with the opposite sex before.

A thought struck. If kissing Declan felt this good, she could only imagine how amazing he would be in bed. The man had mad skills with his tongue, which was presently teasing her mouth open and promising complete and total ecstasy.

What harm could touching his face do? She freed his shirt from her right hand and then ran her finger along his strong jawline.

He groaned again, but this time it came out more like a low growl. It was sexy as all get out, too.

She commanded her heart to slow down. As it was, it threatened to crack her ribs for how fast and hard it beat against her chest. This man was more than temptation on a stick. He was sinning on Sundays delicious. Her blood raced through her veins, warming her from the inside out.

This time, she found the strength to push him away.

He locked gazes with her and tried to pull off a casual smile. "Told you that was dangerous."

What could Declan say? The pull toward
Piper was stronger than anything he'd felt before and
he was losing big time in the willpower game. The heat
between them was beyond anything he'd experienced,
and he was skilled in the hot sex department.

The whole attraction to his best friend thing needed
to be addressed at some point. Right now, he tried to
convince himself they were celebrating the good news
that whoever set her up to take the fall for murder had
failed.

He refocused on the case as he tried to shake off the
attraction thing, and James Bowker immediately came
to mind. Declan reclaimed the driver's seat as Piper
buckled in. He started the engine and navigated onto
the road leading toward COZI.

"I can't help but think the timing of James Bowker
showing up in town while you're being set up to take
a murder charge is suspect." Declan gripped the
steering wheel.

"Same here. But, you know, my dad is gone. What good would it do to put me behind bars. There's nothing he can gain from it," she admitted.

"Revenge can be a powerful motivator," Declan pointed out.

"True. I guess I've never been so angry at a person that I'd want to destroy their life and the lives of the ones they love," she said.

"Greed can do that to an already twisted person." Coming from a family with a lot of money, Declan had seen the way others treated his father, hoping for a handout.

"I don't know him personally but it's safe to say that he hated my father." Now that her father was gone, maybe the man had transferred that hate to her. With her gran's mind slipping, making her an unreliable alibi, it would be easier to target the family.

Declan's phone buzzed, indicating a text was coming in. "Do mind checking it while I'm driving?"

"Not at all."

He fished his cell out of his front pocket and handed it over to her.

"It's from Hawk. He's reminding you about promising to let him borrow your truck for an early morning haul tomorrow. How do you want me to respond?"

"Ask him if we can meet up after we make our next stop." Declan wanted to look Brody Axel in the face when he asked about the petition. If Brody couldn't produce one, Declan had a few choice words for the guy. And, yes, he didn't appreciate the guy for trying to get to know Piper. Declan didn't care if the man was new in town, Piper was off limits.

An annoying little voice reminded him that he had no claim to a relationship with her beyond friends. She was free to date anyone she wanted. Brody Axel was most definitely not her type, though. He wasn't good enough for her and Declan would've made his opinion known to her if the situation called for it. As her friend, there was no way he'd let her go down the wrong dating path.

Well, he had to stop himself right there.

They were good friends because neither crossed certain lines—lines of mutual respect for one another. And no matter how much his heart argued, Declan had no right to tell her who she could date.

"He said he could swing by COZI tonight on the way home from the hospital. Your dad is doing great and asking Hawk to update him on ranch business. Between Hawk and Levi, your dad is covered." She studied the screen before looking up. "How should I reply?"

"Are you good with me sleeping over your house again tonight?" he asked.

"I'd like the company a lot actually."

"We'll be home in a couple of hours. Let him know we'll text him after we get there and he can swing by." He would no doubt bring Miss Penny, considering the two seemed to be a packaged deal. She could handle one of the vehicles.

"Done," she said, self-satisfied as she set the phone on the bench seat between them. "I should check on Gran and see how she's doing with Red. She was barely awake when I went inside her room this morning and was more than happy to agree to spend the day with your sweet pup."

Declan smiled as she made the call. He couldn't help it. Red was part of his family and he liked how much Piper and her grandmother had taken to her. Red seemed smitten with them, too, so the feeling seemed to be mutual.

Brody's place was a small house on half an acre of land down the road from COZI and they were almost there. Piper's phone buzzed in her hand the minute she ended her call. She checked the screen.

"It's the sheriff," she said in a surprised-sounding voice. She blinked a couple of times and took the call. "Hello."

There were a few beats of silence.

"Did you say Clinton Tripp?" Piper listened. "Not that I'm aware of."

More of that silence.

"I can ask Gran, but I can't guarantee anything there," she admitted. "I'll let you know as soon as I speak to her. Thanks for the call."

Declan barely waited for her to hang up before curiosity got the best of him. "What was that about?"

"Do you know Clinton Tripp?" she asked.

"Not very well and what I do know about him says he's a hothead. Why?"

"Apparently, a neighbor says he's been threatening my gran over water rights. She can basically open up a funnel that drains on his property. Some people think he wants to pipe it and sell it to oil companies. But he can't do any of it without her permission," she informed. Water rights and ranching had a long and sometimes sordid past. Lives had been lost over battles for control. "He was also in a fight with Harry Whitaker for the same reason."

"Did the sheriff say whether or not she brought him in for questioning?" he asked.

"No. She couldn't give details. She was trying to get information from me, but Gran hasn't mentioned him so I'm guessing it's just another angle Sheriff Justice is looking into."

"From what I hear, he's a real tool to work with." Declan didn't like the sound of this.

"I need to ask Gran if he's been stopping by or trying to communicate with her. I'd like to give the sheriff access to Gran's cell phone and computer, but I don't have the right to do that and I don't feel good about sneaking around behind her back. How do I ask that of her, Declan? She's always been this smart and feisty person who was larger than life in my eyes. How do I take away her ability to make her own decisions?"

Smart and feisty were two words that Declan would use to describe Piper and they were qualities that he loved in her. Loved?

Yeah, he couldn't deny the truth staring him in the face. He loved Piper. They had history. He chalked it up to that and not the obvious truth that his feelings for her had taken on a life of their own.

"This can't possibly be an easy time and I can't begin to know what you're going through, Piper. So, I won't insult you by pretending." His words were met with a look of appreciation. "I do know a few things. For one, you inherited a lot of your grandmother's feistiness. I think she's probably proud of the fact. I can see it in her eyes when she looks at you."

He pulled onto the side of the road and parked on the shoulder of the street, preferring not to alert Brody Axel to the fact they were about to arrive. And then he continued, "If anyone can find a way to make decisions for your grandmother without taking away her ability to be herself, it's you, Piper."

She reached over and touched his arm. "Do you really believe that?"

"One hundred percent," he confirmed. "There's another benefit. You're home. We might have lost touch before, but I want to stay friends. I want to be there for you and your gran."

"You have your own responsibilities, Declan. You don't have time to go around saving me and Gran."

"The honest truth is that I like being around you. I missed this...us." His admission got his heart racing.

"Same," she said in a voice so quiet he had to strain to hear her.

"Good. Then, let's keep our friendship going this time," he said.

"For how long? Let's face facts. When one of us meets 'the one,' this...us...is over. No spouse is going to want us to stay connected at the hip." She didn't wait for a response. Instead, she rushed out the passenger door.

Words failed and he stupidly let her race toward Brody's house.

PIPER HAD *no idea what had just possessed her to say those words to Declan. They were true. No woman on earth would want the man she was in a relationship with to have such a close friendship with another woman, and vice versa. She and Declan had history and they loved each other. Clearly, it ran deeper than the brother-sister variety considering the heat in the kisses they shared. Those were the problem. If they were like brother and sister, they had a better shot at keeping it going beyond this…whatever this was.*

She was frustrated. She was angry. She was anxious. And she was taking it out on him.

A few deep breaths later, and he caught up to her. "Piper," he started but she put a hand up to stop him.

"I'm sorry, Declan. That was out of bounds," she admitted.

"I do care about you." It went without saying.

"I know."

"Are we okay?" His brow furrowed and concern lines scored his forehead.

"We are. I'm not so much. But I will be." She steeled her resolve. "And even though I may not always show it, I hope you know how much I appreciate everything you're doing for me right now."

"You don't have to—"

"Yes, I do. You've been nothing but kind, so I was out of line snapping at you back there." She could admit that her feelings for him took on a life of their own at times despite her best efforts to reel them in. "Forgive me?"

"You didn't even have to ask," he said, and he wasn't helping. Her attraction to him was already complicating matters to no end. Did he have to be so damn kind and easy to love?

Piper heaved a sigh. He had no plans to keeping her emotions in check easy on her. It was a good thing she was strong. She had to change the subject or risk ruining her friendship—a friendship that she really was grateful for. "Think he'll give us a straight answer?"

"No. But I'll be able to tell a lot about him by the lies he tells."

She restarted her walk down his lane and toward his front door, half expecting a pack of ravenous dogs to attack them at any given second.

Thankfully, no such animals came as they stepped onto the porch of the one-story ranch-style home. It *was modest and, if she remembered correctly, a rental. No big deal except that it meant whoever was here was most likely a temporary resident, someone who might not be invested in the community.*

The old porch creaked and groaned underneath Declan's weight. The whole place could use a fresh coat of paint. Some would describe the home as rustic. She wouldn't disagree with the assessment.

There were various jars and ladders on the porch, and it looked like someone might be ready to start on some updates. Or had started and given up.

Declan knocked on the door.

To be honest, the whole place was strangely quiet. Maybe Piper was used to be at COZI where life flourished between the hanging plants and the birds constantly singing. There was just so much life on the property and in the house. Gran was always humming some tune. She had on her apron and was using her mixer or blender or some kitchen appliance while she practically danced around the kitchen.

There was usually music playing in the background on the radio. The radio. That's how nostalgic Gran's place was. She still turned on the radio. Heck, she still owned one. And no matter how many times Piper tried to get her gran to use a tablet, the woman would just smile and find her station.

Stubborn and rebellious didn't begin to describe her, but she wasn't the kind of person who rubbed people's noses in her decisions. She went about her business without asking permission. And no attempt to bring her into the twenty-first century worked unless she was the one who'd asked for it.

Those memories made Piper smile. She made a note to spend more time thinking about the things about Gran that made her happy. Besides, she reasoned, Gran wasn't gone yet. And it would be a shame to miss out on the time they had left by being constantly sad. The epiphany smacked her in the forehead with the force of a two-by-four. That was what she'd been searching for. That happiness. That gorgeous, fleeting happiness that she'd experienced more times than she could count in COZI's kitchen. With Gran.

Only paying attention to the sad fact that Gran was slowly losing herself would rob them of the time they had left together. And that really would be a shame.

Piper's resolve strengthened just as the door swung open. Brody stood there all brooding and angry looking. His gaze shifted from Piper to Declan, and when it did, his eyes narrowed. Based on his stern expression, he wasn't thrilled with their visit, especially Declan's.

"Can I help you?" Brody's gaze practically bore into Declan.

"As a matter of fact, you can." Declan's voice was a study in calm. "We heard you were gathering names for a petition and we'd—"

"Excuse me…what?"

"The petition for streetlights," Declan explained. "You brought it over to Ms. Gold's house yesterday. My friend and I would like to support the cause by adding our names to it."

Brody shrugged his broad shoulders. His lips disappeared into a thin line. And Piper tried to hide the hurt at hearing herself described as a friend.

"Sorry, man. I can't help you. I have no idea what you're talking about," Brody insisted.

Declan crossed his arms over his chest. "You sure about that?"

"Owen mentioned his boss's mind was slipping. She must have me confused with someone else." He was lying. There was no question in Piper's mind.

The problem was that she couldn't prove it.

16

"**I** guess we best be on our way then." Declan

dropped his hands to his sides, palms toward Brody. The gesture was a show of trust. And in this case, meant to disarm the guy.

"Sorry I couldn't help you out," Brody said.

Declan wouldn't put money on that statement being true. There was no use arguing, though. He also didn't want to tip Brody off more than they just did.

"No problem, man," Declan said. "Next time."

"Yeah."

"Take it easy." He could almost feel the tension rolling off Piper in palpable waves. He could've sworn that he'd felt her muscles stiffen when he'd referred to her as a friend a few seconds ago. It was necessary.

On instinct, he started to reach for her hand but stopped himself in time, thinking it might be best if Brody still believed he had a chance with Piper. He didn't. Plus, the thought of her going out with a guy like him was basically a knife to the chest for Declan. And that made him a huge hypocrite considering he wasn't exactly asking her for a commitment.

Strangely, the idea didn't make him want to loosen the collar around his neck. He'd let that sit for a minute, see what happened when he stirred it later on.

"Sorry for the interruption." He turned and walked away, fully aware of the risk he took in turning his back to Brody. Again, the move was intended to elicit trust. And yet again, he had to stop himself from grabbing Piper's hand. Being in physical contact with her at all times was becoming habit-forming.

The two walked down the lane side-by-side and in silence. He picked up on a mood vibrating from her. One that warned him to tread lightly.

Neither spoke until they reached the pickup and, once inside, there was very little conversation.

"He's guilty of something," Declan said.

"Yes." It was never a good sign when Piper gave a one-word answer.

"I wish we could get reliable information from your grandmother." He tried to get the conversation going again.

"Same."

"Do you think it's possible that he and Clinton Tripp know each other?" This could be about water rights.

She shrugged.

Since pushing her to talk would be as productive as trying to run a till through dry soil, he finished the short drive to COZI without saying another word.

The minute he parked; she was out of the vehicle. Her grandmother was on the back porch, which was easy to see from the private parking area. Red came running toward her as Declan exited the vehicle. She bent down and scratched his dog's ears.

He decided to hold back and wait for Hawk at the vehicle after firing off a text to let him know they were here. Besides, Piper needed space. He'd learned the hard way years ago the more he crowded her when she needed air, the worse her mood became.

That was the art of any relationship. Knowing when to back off and when to step in and listen or provide comfort. It took time to get to know someone on that personal of a level. The two of them had a history that went way back. Despite their long absence from each other's lives, he liked that he could still read her moods. That he knew when to step in and when to step back.

This was a step back moment.

Declan had personal information to process on his own. Like the fact that his father was awake and headed toward recovery. Declan had been so concerned with Piper's situation that he hadn't allowed that relief to flood him.

The circumstances surrounding his uncle were more complicated. But at least his father would be able to give his statement now and clear up, once and for all, what really happened in the equipment room. The sheriff's interview skills were top-notch. She'd get to the bottom of it.

Once the person conspiring against Piper was put behind bars, Declan's life—a life that had been upended for months while his father was in a coma—could start some semblance of normalcy again.

For so many reasons, most of them to do with his cousins, Declan could only pray that Uncle Donny had nothing to do with the accident. His uncle had done some questionable things in his life. Declan couldn't imagine the aftershock that would follow attempting to murder his brother. Reed, Cage and the others didn't deserve a father who was capable of killing to get his way.

The ranch would be divided equally among Clive McGannon's children, and that included his five bonus sons, who were Donny's kids. The only gain Donny could have in the ranch being divided up was the possibility he could work his children into giving him pieces of their shares.

It was a questionable strategy. And yet, Declan couldn't be certain his uncle wouldn't. The sad reality was a gut punch to someone who prized family above all else.

The sound of gravel spewing underneath tires pulled him out of his thoughts. He looked up in time to see Miss Penny waving. Hawk pulled up next to Declan's pickup. He exchanged quick greetings before handing over keys.

After a quick round of hugs, Declan headed inside the house.

Red greeted him at the door and, figuring he'd been neglecting her in the past twenty-four hours, he took her outside and threw a ball with her in the backyard. She was young enough to have pent up energy that needed working out.

Piper eventually called out to them to tell them to come eat. Declan obliged, feeding his dog first before seating himself at the table. One look at her and he could tell she'd been able to conquer her anger except that another wall had come up between them. All signs of frustration were gone. Her face was blank, like when he'd first seen her.

Why did he want to be the one to reach her again? Why did he need to feel a connection that was *dangerous for both of them? Why did his heart sink when he looked at her and realized she'd shut him out?*

PIPER FINISHED *her meal and did dishes alongside Declan. He was in one of his quiet, reflective moods and it didn't bother her. It was nice, in fact, to know someone so well that all she had to do was take one look at him and she could read his mood. Shared history was powerful. Friendship was powerful. And she prayed those things would be powerful enough to stem the blow-burn attraction sizzling between them.*

All they needed was a little time to get used to being together to douse the embers. And no more kissing.

Declan yawned. His third time while doing dishes side-by-side.

"I'm thinking of calling it an early evening tonight. What do you think?" she asked, trying to give him an out because she knew he'd feel a responsibility to stay up with her as long as she was awake.

"Whatever you want to do is fine by me." This time, his voice was unreadable. She chalked it up to him being tired. Plus, the simple truth that it had been

another long day that seemed stacked with endless responsibilities.

"I never saw guests arrive," Declan pointed out.

"Wrong week. I was able to get into COZI's e-mail earlier to check and Gran had the wrong date." More evidence Gran's memory was failing faster than Piper wanted. The good news was that she was here now. She could help.

Piper excused herself to shower and by the time she stepped out of the bathroom, Declan had beat her to the punch. One of the many benefits of having more than one shower in the house. Jeans hung low on his hips, a stray bead of water rolled down his chest. Her eyes followed the trail until she reminded herself to look away before he caught her.

"Does Red need to go out?" she asked. The sweet girl had curled up on a chair in the bedroom.

"All taken care of," he said.

They climbed into bed at the same time, him on top of the covers. Tonight, she didn't think it was a good idea to snuggle up next to him. He seemed like he needed space.

So, she was surprised when he reached over to her and pulled her over. She willingly complied, settling into her favorite place in the world—the crook of his arm.

The next thing she knew, she was out.

A THUMP FOLLOWED by barking shocked Piper awake. Declan was first to move. He was up and out faster than she could peel her covers off.

The noise came from downstairs. Piper worried that Gran had fallen trying to get up the stairs, berating herself for not having made provisions for such a scenario. But the heart wrenching yelp that came next from Red warned this situation was far more serious.

Already in the hallway, she backtracked to retrieve her phone on the nightstand. Pulse pounding, fingers shaking, she managed to call 911 and asked for help.

"Find a hiding spot and stay there until I come for you," Declan's voice boomed upstairs, freezing her to her spot. One hand on the railing and halfway down, she mentally debated listening to him or continuing her descent.

The fact she hadn't heard a noise or shout out from Gran worried her. Then, there was the yelp. Her heart literally burst for Red. If anything happened to her…

Piper couldn't even go there. She'd never been one to fall into the category of too-stupid-to-live and she had no plans to start now. But going upstairs and hiding when she might actually be able to help didn't seem like the best play, either.

Going down to the first floor via the stairs was a bad idea. On the second floor, there was a trellis right outside the lavender bedroom window. She could climb down and assess the situation. Possibly even create a diversion.

There was no way she planned to lock herself inside a closet and hope for the best. Declan was trying to protect her. She understood his reasoning for wanting her to stay put. Except that if anything happened to him, she'd be a sitting duck.

The 911 dispatcher had reassured help was on the way, but the closest deputy was half an hour away and the sheriff was about the same. Thirty minutes. A lot could happen in that timeframe. There might not be anyone left to save at that point.

Piper ducked into the lavender bedroom, named for the paint color and the fact that Gran always put fresh flowers when a guest stayed over. Back in the day, it had been widely requested. Admittedly, the rooms could use some updating but the lavender room was one of her favorites.

She opened the window and climbed out, gripping the solid wood so hard her knuckles went white. Step by step, she lowered herself. With bare feet, she was able to cling onto each wood slat, but she would pay the price later. She'd already collected a splinter in the pad of her right foot. It hurt but there was no time to worry about it. Adrenaline spiked, covering the pain and keeping her moving.

As she passed beside a first-floor window, she glanced inside. The door was open, and a small glow came from the hallway lights. Gran had always insisted guests should be able to see inside the house day or night. The nightlights created a soft glow and would come in very useful now.

Gran's room was on the other side of the house, as was the living room and kitchen. This was the side with bedrooms. Piper tried the window only to find it locked. She expected that.

How could she re-enter the house without drawing attention to herself?

The backdoor? Only if it was unlocked.

She would have to figure out how the intruder came inside. Following his tracks would be the easiest way. At least, she hoped he was alone. If there was more than one, she was going to be in serious trouble.

Hopping off the lattice, she landed right on the splinter. Her leg drew up automatically and she hopped around a couple of times on the soft grass. So much for adrenaline covering all the pain. It helped. What was it about feet and pain? Why was it the worst?

Taking in a couple of breaths, she eased her foot down and hobbled on her heel. Keeping her body as flush with the house as she could, she moved through the flower beds against the building. Slowing her breathing to as close to normal as she could under the circumstances, she turned the corner to the back of the house.

Piper scanned the tree line, made visible by the barn lighting. Her heart pounded painfully against her ribs and her throat went completely dry at the memory from yesterday. So, why didn't someone come in guns blazing?

Why did someone come inside at all?

Glancing over at the parking pad as she made her way toward the back porch, she could think of one good reason. Declan's truck was gone. The hairs on the back of her neck pricked. Someone most likely had been keeping an eye on the house. Did the killer intend to remove a witness…her?

She tried to calm her racing heart as she moved toward the back door. The window had been broken and someone had simply and easily reached inside to unlock the lock.

Normally, security wasn't an issue in a town like Cattle Cove where most folks still left their keys inside their vehicles and wouldn't think of locking a door at home. Times had changed and there'd been a recent rise in local crimes—a trend that had Gran locking the doors to COZI every night.

From there, she heard grunting noises and then a crash. Gran was quiet. Piper hadn't heard from her and that was causing a whole heap of anxiety as she slipped through the kitchen toward the sound of the grunts. At the last minute, she detoured to check on Gran in her room. Every fiber of her being needed to be in that living room, but she moved cautiously because she didn't want to make things worse.

Then, she heard Declan mutter a curse and that caused her heart to drop to her toes and her course to reverse. He was in trouble. She glanced around for something…anything to use as a weapon once back in the kitchen. Her eye stopped on the cast iron skillet Gran always left on the stove.

Piper grabbed it by the handle and beat feet into the living room, praying whoever was in there would be too busy fighting Declan to notice her. Her guess was on the money. The guy was big as an ox as he wrestled around on the floor with Declan.

Brody.

17

Declan took an elbow to the face and his lip busted open. That was going to hurt in the morning. He grunted and struggled for purchase on Brody's chest, digging his fingers in between the man's rib cage.

It was Brody's turn to curse. He was strong but Declan had the kind of endurance that would wear the guy out. Brody was a sprinter, quick punches, jabs and knee thrusts. Declan was a long-distance runner, built to go the distance.

He felt the trickle of blood from his bottom lip. The swelling would come next. In the meantime, he planned to inflict a couple of bruises on Brody in return. In fact, he drew back his fist and then slammed it into Brody's jaw. The move hurt Declan like hell but that was nothing compared to what Brody probably just felt. For him, it was a lot like being hit by a two-by-four.

Brody's head snapped back. He grunted in pain. When his head righted itself again, he had to shake it to get his bearings. His gaze unfocused, he looked to be *struggling to stay lucid. And since opportunities had been few and far between in this fight, Declan capitalized on the moment. His fist was already in motion when he realized he'd been too eager.*

Brody caught the jab and twisted Declan's wrist until it felt like it might snap. Declan dropped to his knees as he lifted his other arm and then dropped his elbow down, breaking Brody's grip.

Popping up, Declan tried to pivot. Nope. Didn't work. An opportunity came to headbutt Brody. He anticipated the move. Dammit. It was too obvious, and Brody was about to be punished for it. Brody caught hold of Declan's arm and rolled. The guy was a tank and all two-hundred-plus pounds of him landed on Declan's forearm. At least, that's the way it felt. And now Declan was at a momentary disadvantage.

Right up until something—a frying pan?—landed upside Brody's head. The man growled as his head snapped to the side.

The move gave Declan enough leverage to roll on top of Brody, tucking his arms to his sides. With powerful thighs, Declan squeezed. He fired off a few punches, hoping to knock the guy out long enough to tie him up.

Sirens sounded in the distance at the time he realized the person behind the blow to Brody's head was Piper. Declan smiled as he delivered a knock-out punch.

He took a few seconds to catch his breath. "He's out but stay back. He's strong and it would be a mistake to underestimate him."

"I have to check on Gran." She ran out of the room while Declan held tight to Brody. She was back in two shakes. "She's shaken up, but she'll be okay."

Piper flipped on the lamp, bathing the room in light.

And that's when he heard the whimper.

"Red," Piper said after scanning the room.

Declan had been so caught up in trying to diffuse Brody that he hadn't had a chance to look for his pup. Piper's expression caused his heart to break in half.

She locked onto a lump in between the coffee table and the sofa. A red lump. A lump that wasn't moving.

"Oh, baby." Piper's voice sent anger rushing through him as water gathered in his eyes.

Nothing could happen to Red. Declan was supposed to protect her like he'd promised when he scooped her in his arms on that hot Texas morning. He'd given her his word that he would never let anything happen to her again.

And he'd failed.

Moisture blurred his eyes and white-hot anger flared through him. "What's happening over there?"

"She's hurt, Declan. Who do I call?"

He rattled off the number to his vet, Derek Jacobs. "Where is she hurt?"

"I'm not sure. It looks like it hurts her to move." Those words were worse than a physical punch.

"Don't try." He didn't want the situation to be worse.

She called the vet's personal number and got an answer immediately. She quickly and succinctly relayed the details along with COZI's address. Then, she turned her attention toward Declan. "He's on his way."

The sirens blazed outside as Piper called the sheriff next. "Brody Axel is being subdued in our living room. He came through the back door."

A few seconds later, Sheriff Justice entered the room from the back of the house, her weapon drawn. She locked onto Brody and Declan.

"He's starting to wake up," Declan said, wanting to see the bastard talk his way out of this. But all he could really think about in the moment was Red.

Brody shook his head again and tried to blink his eyes open. Too late. Sheriff Justice was there, rolling him onto his stomach and drawing his hands behind his back, cuffing him.

Declan pushed up from his knees, the force of the blows he'd taken were starting to let him know just how much pain he was going to be in later. Nothing mattered more than Red and there was one more person he needed to see for himself despite the reassurance from Piper that her Gran was going to be fine.

Piper seemed to shift gears at the same time he moved to Red. Declan dropped down on his knees as anger swirled through him like a swell. The storm brewing was about to be devastating and Declan wished he'd realized what had happened to Red before the sheriff had arrived. Brody would be in a lot worse shape than he was now.

Brody needed to be locked away for the rest of his life.

"I didn't do it," Brody said as Piper disappeared toward her gran's room.

"Let me know what's happening in there," Declan shouted. Brody's words didn't sit well.

"Do what?" the sheriff asked, right after reading Brody his rights.

"Kill that dude." There was a hint of desperation in Brody's voice now.

"Who did, Mr. Axel?" the sheriff's voice was a study in calm.

"Owen Dyer," Brody immediately said. "He's behind all of this. He promised Clinton Tripp that he'd get a signature from the old lady, and he said we had an opportunity to take her property in the process. Until that bitch showed up."

"Where is Mr. Dyer now?" Sheriff Justice asked.

"At my house," he supplied.

"Was he ever out of state? I already knew that he lied about his mother. She's been gone for three years," Justice supplied.

"No. He's been hiding in my spare bedroom and my attic if someone comes by," he informed.

"Is he there now?" she continued.

"Yes. Go see for yourself."

The sheriff redirected one of her deputies and all Declan could think was how both of these men needed to be locked away. "What makes Mr. Dyer believe he can have the B&B?"

"Everything. He convinced Ms. Gold to name him as successor to Piper. He couldn't kill the bitch outright because that would be too obvious. But he could have her locked away for murder and take over the property from Ms. Gold since she was about to be declared incompetent," Brody confessed.

"And you'll swear to this under oath?"

"I will. But only if I can get a deal," Brody said.

"I never offered a deal." Based on the sheriff's tone, he would rot behind bars before she would help him out.

PIPER HELPED Gran into the living room where Declan was hunkered over Red. Her heart bled for the sweet pup. "Gran is here. She's okay. You wanted to see for yourself."

Hair disheveled, shoulders rounded, Gran showed signs of distress.

"I'm shaken up, but otherwise fine," Gran admitted.

"She walked in here on her own. I'm literally just here for backup," Piper said.

"Brody Axel," Gran said quietly as he was being walked out the front door.

"Actually, Owen Dyer is behind this whole scenario. He wanted Piper behind bars to he could inherit COZI," Declan explained.

The sheriff returned a few minutes later alongside the family vet, Derick Jacobs. Declan didn't budge, so Piper moved beside him and put her hand on his shoulder.

"I'll put on a pot of tea," Gran said, looking like she needed something to do to keep busy.

Piper was starting a mental list of things they'd need to do tonight to secure the house. One of them was board up the glass. She could order a new door in the morning.

The vet examined Red. He looked to Declan and said, "The good news is she's young and strong. She should make a full recovery. The bad news is I'd like to take her into my office to examine her. Just to be sure. I'll want to observe her for a couple of days."

"I'm there and I hope you have a cot I can sleep on," Declan said.

"That's not ne—"

"Yes, it is. I made a promise to her that I would always be by her side and I'm a man of my word." The way Declan said those words, the vet would be crazy to argue. He seemed to know it, too.

"I'll make arrangements."

"I don't need much. I can sleep in a chair if I have to. I'm not leaving her alone," Declan's voice radiated strength and his words struck Piper at the core.

"Same here," Piper said. "I want to go, too."

She glanced toward the kitchen, torn between being home for her gran and being by Red's side as she went through what would be a scary couple of nights.

"I can make a call and get coverage for your grandmother," Declan offered. "Any one of my brothers or cousins would be here in a heartbeat."

"That seems like a big imposition," she started to argue but he stopped her by taking her hand in his.

"It's what we do for each other. Remember? We don't shut each other out when times are tough, we circle the wagons and help each other even more. Okay? And we need to get that splinter out of your foot." The sincerity in his eyes, the softness in his voice made it impossible to argue.

"I'll just ask Gran if she minds."

"Minds what?" Gran entered the room from the hallway to the kitchen.

"Red needs medical attention at the vet's office," Piper started.

"Go. Off with you," Gran swatted at Piper like she was shooing a fly.

"I hate to leave you, Gran." The vet handed over a few sterile supplies and Declan removed the splinter from her foot.

"Me? I'm fine. Go on."

Next, Declan was on his cell, texting. The response was almost immediate. "Jack's on his way. I'll just make sure he knows to board up that window."

Piper's heart was full. She wasn't practiced at accepting help from others but it sure beat carrying the whole load on her shoulders. It was a nice feeling and warmth spread through her. For the first time since hearing about Gran's condition, Piper felt like she wasn't alone.

"There's one more thing," Declan said as the vet listened to Red's vital signs. He looked at Piper and took her hand in his. "I don't want this to end. Ever. You've been my best friend for longer than I can remember. I know we parted ways for a few years but seeing you again reminded me of what love and friendship really means. I guess what I'm saying is that I love you, Piper."

Tears filled her eyes. Not tears of sadness but tears of joy.

"I love you, too, Declan."

"Then, why wait another minute? I feel like we've wasted enough time apart and with my dad's situation I've realized just how quickly life can change. In a blink, we can lose people we love. Another second later, and they're back. No one knows what tomorrow will look like. I've never been more reminded of the fact. So, I don't want to waste another second of my life being without you."

"Are you asking what I think you are, Declan McGannon?" Shock didn't begin to cover her reaction, but something was bigger, something grounded her.

And that something was love. "Because if you don't ask, I will."

His smile was ear-to-ear.

"Piper Gold, will you do me the incredible honor of marrying me?"

"Yes, Declan. I will marry you. I promise to be your equal partner and to love you for the rest of my life."

Declan stood, pulling her into an embrace. He kissed her. Soft and tender at first, and then hard and bruising and territorial after.

Piper pulled back and looked into the eyes of the man she loved, of the man she had always loved and would always love. With him, she found her spot. She found home. And never again would she feel alone.

J ack McGannon opened the door to the vet's office and walked in. Voices from exam room two echoed into the empty lobby. He recognized them as his brother, Declan, and his new fiancée, Piper.

"Hello in there," Jack called out, not wanting to catch anyone off guard. Honestly, folks in Cattle Cove had been jumpy lately ever since a crime wave started winding its way through the town's once-safe streets. He couldn't blame them.

"Come on in," Declan answered.

On the drive over, Jack prepared himself to see Red lying on the exam table with tubes sticking out of her. Walking in, he found the opposite. Tail wagging, she hurried over to greet him with a slight limp.

"Good, girl." He crouched down to her level to give her a good scratch behind the ears. Animals were so much easier to deal with than people, he thought. They wear their emotions on the outside. People were far *more complex. He glanced up at his brother, "Other than the limp, is she okay?"*

"Bruised a few ribs, but, yeah, she's going to be fine." Declan practically beamed.

Jack stood up and walked over to his brother, bringing him into a bear hug. He couldn't say he'd ever seen his brother this happy and it had everything to do with the person standing beside him. "Good to see you again, Piper."

"Same to you, Jack." She beamed almost as much as Declan. The two were crazy in love and it showed. Jack figured he better make this visit quick before any of that nonsense rubbed off on him. He'd had it in a bad way for someone. She apparently didn't feel the same way, considering she ran off with another guy. Last Jack heard she was engaged. Not a memory he cared to relive.

In fact, he'd been able to shove those thoughts down deep and tuck them away until recently. Several of his brothers had found the kind of happiness Jack had been fool enough to believe he had with his ex.

Shaking his head, he did his level best to shake loose of those thoughts—thoughts that took him down a path of regret.

Besides, even if Natalie came back begging—and rest assured she would not—he didn't do second chances. Once burned twice shy. Basic survival skills kicked in and his had done a good job of keeping him alive so far. They would also keep him from ever speaking to her again.

"Thanks for stopping by on your way home from the hospital." Declan's voice cut through the fog.

"Yeah, no problem. Figured you'd want to hear it straight." Everyone hoped Uncle Donny wasn't responsible for the accident that had left their dad in a coma.

"What does Dad say about what happened?" Declan asked.

"He doesn't remember any of the accident." Jack still called it an accident for lack of a better word because the other one that came to mind was crime. It was probably wishful thinking on his part and out of love for his cousins that Jack didn't want the latter to be true. "But here's the thing, when the sheriff mentioned Uncle Donny...Dad flinched."

Jack turned to Piper and said, "By the way, welcome to the family."

TO KEEP READING Jack's story, click here.

COWBOY RESCUE

BONUS - CHAPTER ONE

Jack McGannon leaned a hip against the side of his pickup truck, then crossed his legs at his ankles. He fished his cell from the front pocket of his jeans, questioning why he'd volunteered to take this assignment. Traffic had been a nightmare on the highway. Weather was moving in. Seeing the condition of the mares he was about to rescue was going to be a gut punch.

This so-called animal sanctuary became a prison after the owner retired, turning the family business over to a son who couldn't care less about the animals, the property, or the house from the looks of it. There had to be a special place in hell for folks who abused or neglected innocent animals.

The storm brewing outside had nothing on Jack's mood, which was darkening by the minute. But then he hadn't been in the right mindset since receiving an unsettling text from one of his exes yesterday.

Jack fisted his free hand, thinking he definitely should have taken a pass on this one.

Before he could thumb through his contacts for Texas Parks and Wildlife, Warden William Sparks came around the side of the seventies ranch-style home. In his late thirties, most would describe him as tall and lanky with a runner's build. He stared at the ground, a scowl on his face.

The second he glanced up and saw Jack, he heaved a sigh and managed a smile. It was then Jack saw something move on the front porch. From this distance, he couldn't tell what it was.

"Afternoon, William," Jack said to his law enforcement division contact.

"Afternoon?" William cocked an eyebrow and glanced at his watch. He looked official in his department-issued all brown uniform. "I've barely had breakfast."

Jack chuckled and shook the man's hand. He guessed to some folks ten a.m. qualified as morning. "Activity starts on the ranch at four, so, yeah, ten feels late."

"Well, I guess there's probably a lot of truth to that but for us 'normal' folk, ten o'clock is still squarely in the morning."

"I haven't seen ten o'clock as a morning in…" He laughed. "Probably my entire life."

He was a natural fit for early mornings but there were parts of being a McGannon that weren't so natural. Like the whole being perfect part or when it made him a target for someone looking to cash in on his name.

"Good to see you again," William said, his tone serious now.

"How long has it been?" Jack didn't normally volunteer for pickups. He usually waited for the animals to arrive at the ranch and then rolled up his sleeves to help.

"My people are rounding up the mares. These are the last two of the bunch. My office appreciates your help in taking in animals, or finding homes for them." Jack made eye contact and held it. "I'll warn you. These two are emaciated. I can count their ribs and see their hip bones..." William took a few seconds before continuing. It was obvious how much he cared about animals. "They've been started on good quality hay in small quantity and have been given oral electrolytes and probiotics."

"I don't understand some people." Jack gestured toward the broken-down ranch-style home. Volunteering to be the one to pick up the pair of mares had given him an excuse to be off property and in the northern Austin area.

"That makes two of us." William shook his head. "But these horses just hit the ranching jackpot, if you don't mind my saying. They'll be treated like royalty from here on out."

Jack personally planned to see to it. The family vet had already been alerted and would be ready to go once Jack got the mares home.

"Hold tight," William said. "I'll bring the horses around."

Jack moved behind his trailer, opened it up and set up the ramp for the mares. He glanced over at the porch again. A dog? He took a couple of steps closer to get a better look. Thick fur and a hot Texas sun weren't exactly friends. This one looked like a Bernese Mountain and Rottweiler mix. The guy barely lifted his head up despite looking like he'd been fed. That part was a relief. Too many times animals came to the ranch that had been nearly starved to death like the mares.

William brought the horses around, so Jack turned around and moved to the trailer. True to William's word, the mares were pitiful looking. More of that anger surfaced. Jack worked to contain it.

After loading them, he closed the back doors and slid the lock to secure them. He needed to get them back to the ranch where Derek Jacobs would be waiting.

The Bernese mix lay dutifully on the porch.

"What's going to happen to that one?" He nodded toward the animal.

"I reckon he'll go to the shelter. It's not ideal and you know how much I hate taking them there," William said.

The dog moved and Jack saw a glint of metal. "What's that on him?"

"Chains. Sydney has my bolt cutters." William barely finished his sentence before Jack stalked to the pickup. He opened up the toolbox and grabbed his Kobalt fourteen-inch cutters.

"No. No. No. I'll take him with me. Maybe the familiarity of the horses and ranch life will give him comfort." The Bernese looked so sad. And maybe it was just that same internal brokenness that Jack could identify with that made him feel a draw to the animal. Either way, whether the Bernese wanted to spend the rest of his days resting and lounging around or working, it didn't matter a bit to Jack. He went into it for the long haul.

Before William could respond, Jack was stalking toward the chained-up animal. He muttered a few curses as he walked straight up to the animal.

"Might be tough to get him to move. I get the sense he's been living on that porch for most of his life," William stated. "And he'll most certainly have fleas.

You sure you want to deal with that on your ride home?"

"He's been through enough already. I'll cope with the fleas if I can give him a better life." Fleas could be dealt with. Walking away from a dog that was chained on a porch wasn't something Jack could live with. He took a risk in getting up close and personal with a strange dog. The Bernese looked defeated. More of that anger surfaced.

"Just checking," William said. "Plus, I had a feeling you'd say something like that. I don't think he's moved since we've been here."

"Is he old?" Jack positioned the cutters and then with a grunt, sliced through the chain.

"Doesn't seem so. As you can see, he is gentle, though. A vet could give a better idea of his age, but I wouldn't say that he's much older than four or five. It can't help being left out here in the heat. And his fur is matted."

"Nothing a little shampoo can't cure." Same as with the fleas. It'd be easy enough to wash him. Jack might not know what to do about the texts from his ex, but animals were second nature to him. He called to the dog to gauge how difficult it was going to be to get the Bernie to move.

The guy didn't even lift his head up.

"Hey, boy." Jack's chest took a hit when the saddest brown eyes stared up at him. The dog's head didn't move but his tail wagged, and that was a good sign.

Considering his ears didn't rear back and his disposition didn't change one bit, Jack had a lot of confidence in moving forward. True enough, up close his hair was matted. And, yes, there would be fleas. Jack had no doubts about it. A quick flea dip would help with those.

Jack fished his cell from his pocket. He snapped a pic of the Bernese and sent it to Derek, alerting him to a need for a once-over on the animal. Those eyes would haunt him forever, especially if he walked away.

"Hey, buddy," he started after replacing his phone. "How about you come home with me? What do you think?"

He searched for any signs of life in the dog and was heartbroken when the animal seemed ready to accept whatever happened. His spirit had to be pretty broken to allow that.

The Bernese didn't have on a collar, just a chain around his neck. Since all the other animals had been seized from the property based on neglect, it was an easy case to justify taking him home to the ranch.

Getting him to stand up of his own free will was important to Jack. It would also rule out any physical injuries that might need to be looked at right away.

Derek was on notice and would make sure all the necessary supplies were available. But the dog wasn't budging.

What Jack needed was a treat. Since he didn't carry around a treat bag in his pocket, he figured a pinch of meat from the sandwich Miss Penny had packed and insisted he bring would have to do. He could pinch off a piece or two of ham and see if he could get the dog to follow him to the truck. Normally, Jack drove a Jeep. This truck belonged to the ranch and was the best hookup for the trailer.

It had a big sticker on the back that said *McGannon Herd*, which he didn't use for his personal vehicle. Being a McGannon already placed a big enough target on his back. He didn't feel the need to blast his whereabouts. It was also the reason he didn't have any social media accounts. Not that he was the type to use them. Jack needed to be outside. He'd rather have reins in his hands than a device. He needed to breathe fresh air and feel the sunshine on his face. And right now, he needed to head back to the truck and grab that sandwich.

"No luck?"

Jack shook his head as he opened the passenger door.

"I have a secret weapon, though." The still fresh sandwich was right where he left it.

A few seconds later, he was within spitting distance of the Bernese...holding out a treat. Bernie seemed like a good name. Yeah, Jack liked that name. "What do you think? Bernie?"

Bernie with the big brown eyes didn't have much in the way of a response. So, Jack held out the bit he pinched off within a foot of the big guy's nose. And...nothing.

Jack flattened his right hand and held it even closer, so the dog could get a good whiff in case the wind had shifted. The move got Bernie's attention. Head to one side, he licked Jack's hand, then nibbled the bite.

"Good boy, Bernie." He needed to get used to his new name. New name for a new life.

Jack tore off another pea-sized treat. Bernie got the hang of this quickly, scooting closer to Jack's hand this time.

"Do you want more?" Jack took a step back and pinched off another piece. He held it on the palm of his hand.

Bernie moved, forcing himself to stand with what looked like great effort. Possible hip dysplasia, Jack thought. It wasn't uncommon in extra-large dogs. Leaving it untreated was akin to abuse. Jack had every bit of understanding for folks who couldn't afford veterinary care; his mother had started a charity for those situations. And there were rescue operations that would help; there was literally no reason to leave a dog to suffer with all the resources out there. And, sometimes, surrender was the kindest option. This place, though, was riddled with neglect.

White-hot anger tore through Jack at the animal's suffering. He also had a dilemma. He could open the trailer and put the ramp down, so Bernie could load up in the back. Or, he could risk picking Bernie up to place him in the passenger seat.

The trailer was a four-stall, and the horses were secured in the front two. Jack didn't like the idea of Bernie being back there even though it would help with the flea problem later. He could make a bed out of horse blankets, but Bernie could end up being jostled around. The other idea was a little riskier.

"Hold on there." William caught onto Jack's plan.

"I won't push him. If he doesn't want me picking him up, I won't do it." Jack had left the passenger door open. He glanced at William. "Do you mind grabbing a couple of blankets from the backseat and making a bed for him on the passenger side?"

"Sure thing." William did the favor.

"Thank you."

"Be careful with him. We both know a hurt animal is cap—"

"He's fine. Promise. I won't do anything stupid." He moved closer to Bernie. "Hey, buddy. All I want to do is get you safely inside the truck. What do you think about it?"

Given Bernie's sheer size, he could deliver a sharp bite. Jack had no intention of needing rabies shots. The image of a long needle in his stomach took hold, causing his body to shiver involuntarily. He had no idea if rabies shots still required those needles and had no intention of finding out today.

As long as he was careful, and Bernie wasn't giving any signs of agitation, Jack could move forward. The dog would only bite out of fear or protection. It was plain to see this guy didn't have a mean bone in his body. Jack managed to maneuver close enough to secure a hand underneath Bernie's front section. All that got was a face lick. Good response.

"Almost there," he soothed. It was the hindquarters he worried about. He used as calm and consistent voice as he could, knowing full well animals often took their cues from humans. Especially domestic animals. "You're doing great."

Scooping the dog up, Jack tensed, half-expecting the worst. He moved quickly to the vehicle and placed Bernie on top of the folded blankets. He eased his hands out from underneath the hefty animal.

"Ever think about changing professions?" William blew out a breath like he'd been holding it the entire walk over.

"Nope."

"If you ever do, my office could use a few good people like you." William was only half-joking, based on the knowing look he gave.

"You know me. Ranching's in the blood. Animals are part of the job." While most ranchers used trucks to herd cattle and ATVs to check fences, McGannon Herd Cattle Ranch still rode horses. A few of the hands had converted to electronic or gas-powered, but Clive McGannon was a renaissance man. He'd taught his sons and nephews the old-fashioned way and they'd embraced it. There was something about starting his day in the saddle that righted the world.

"Hope this creep gets locked away for a long time." Jack nodded toward the house. There were a few choice words that came to mind, words much stronger than creep. Jack bit his tongue.

"We should be solid on this one."

Jack clenched his back teeth. William wasn't lying. Jack could literally count the mares' ribs as he'd loaded them. Disgusting. His faith in humanity was at an all-time low at the moment.

"You're good to come all the way out here, Jack," William said.

"Don't start that kind of rumor. You'll ruin my bad-boy reputation," Jack teased. He wasn't so sure about the good part. He stuck his right hand out between him and William, who took it and gave a good shake.

"It'll kill your dating life," William shot back.

Too soon, Jack thought. Besides, he'd done a great job of that on his own and the comment stung more than he wanted it to. He walked over to the driver's seat, climbed in, and was back on the road toward home where he belonged a minute later.

There weren't a lot of vehicles on this stretch of road, so seeing a hitchhiker out here caught his eye. She had on jean shorts and a tan-colored cotton shirt with her cowgirl boots. Her long legs weren't the only things that he noticed. She wore a wide-brimmed hat that looked incredibly familiar. Boots and a backpack never looked better on a person. Thick, wavy hair that fell halfway down her back blew in the breeze.

Out of nowhere, she turned and tucked her hand in her pocket.

Pulling up beside her, he asked, "Natalie?"

AUTHOR'S NOTE

If you enjoyed this book, I'd be deeply grateful if you'd consider leaving a review on the book retailer/site of your choice. Reviews are so very important to authors (they mean so very much!) and they help other readers find our books.

If you'd like to keep up with new releases, and/or my general thoughts, you can find me on Facebook and my blog. You can also sign up for my newsletter at BarbHan.com.

ALSO BY BARB HAN

Cowboys of Cattle Cove

Cowboy Reckoning

Cowboy Cover-up

Cowboy Retribution

Cowboy Judgment

Cowboy Conspiracy

Cowboy Rescue

Cowboy Target

Cowboy Redemption

Cowboy Intrigue

Cowboy Ransom

Rescue Ridge

Stalked at Rescue Ridge

Targeted at Rescue Ridge

Murder at Rescue Ridge

Captive at Rescue Ridge

Mystery at Rescue Ridge

Crisis at Rescue Ridge

Redemption at Rescue Ridge

Don't Mess With Texas Cowboys

For more of Barb's books, visit www.BarbHan.com.

ABOUT THE AUTHOR

Barb Han is a USA TODAY and Publisher's Weekly Bestselling Author. Reviewers have called her books "gripping" and "heartfelt."

Barb lives in Texas—her true north—with her adventurous family, a Scottish terrier/poodle mix, and a spunky rescue who is often referred to as a hot mess. She is the proud owner of too many books (if there is such a thing). When not writing, she can be found exploring new cities, on a mountain either hiking or skiing depending on the season, or swimming in her own backyard.

Sign up for Barb's newsletter at www.BarbHan.com.